ROCKET GIRLS

HOUSUKE NOJIRI

ROCKET GIRLS

HOUSUKE NOJIRI

TRANSLATED BY JOSEPH REEDER

HAIKA
SORU

SAN FRANCISCO

Rocket Girls
© 1995 Housuke Nojiri, Muttri Moony
First published in Japan in 1995 by Fujimishobo Co., Ltd., Tokyo.
English translation rights arranged with KADOKAWA SHOTEN Publishing Co.,
Ltd., Tokyo.

English translation © 2010 VIZ Media, LLC
Cover art by Katsuya Terada

HAIKASORU
Published by
VIZ Media, LLC
295 Bay Street
San Francisco, CA 94133

www.haikasoru.com

Nojiri, Housuke, 1961-
[Roketto Garu. English]
Rocket girls / Housuke Nojiri ; translated by Joseph Reeder.
p. cm.
"First published in 1995 by Fujimishobo, Co., Ltd., Tokyo."
Translated from the Japanese.
ISBN 978-1-4215-3642-2
I. Reeder, Joseph. II. Title.
PL873.5.O52R6313 2010
895.6'36--dc22

2010019268

The rights of the author of the work in this publication to be so identified have been
asserted in accordance with the Copyright, Designs and Patents Act 1988. A CIP
catalogue record for this book is available from the British Library.

Printed in the U.S.A.
First printing, September 2010

CONTENTS

Chapter I
Yukari Morita: 37 kg, Excellent Health   7

Chapter II
So Easy a Monkey Could Do It   31

Chapter III
Girl of the Jungle   52

Chapter IV
The Fear Diet   72

Chapter V
Perfect by Redesign   93

Chapter VI
Midnight Interview   116

Chapter VII
Endless Countdown   138

Chapter VIII
Meddling Spirits   160

Chapter IX
The Blue Planet Awaits   183

CHAPTER I

YUKARI MORITA: 37 KG, EXCELLENT HEALTH

[ACT 1]

A LONE SILVER tower stood above the white sand and coconut palms of the beach.

Two kilometers away, the image of the launchpad Isao Nasuda was peering at through his binoculars shimmered like a mirage. A fine white mist of liquid oxygen rose off the body of the rocket and spilled steadily down toward the ground.

"Hardly a breath of wind," Isao muttered. "That's good."

The man next to him lowered his own binoculars. "What, Mr. Nasuda? A brisk wind all it takes to topple your rockets these days?" The man was stationed in Indonesia where he worked for the Overseas Economic Cooperation Fund. He had just flown out to the islands. "Don't misunderstand me. No one would like to see this succeed more than I would." His face split into a smile. "What's the saying? Sixth time's the charm?"

Isao snorted. "Accidents happen—goes hand in hand with breaking in new technology. We're in this for the long haul."

The man from the OECF shook his head. "The taxpayers are starting to ask if this is money—and it is a *lot* of money—well spent. It wasn't all that long ago the people out here in the Solomons were running around hunting heads. How is a rocket like this going to help them?"

"Education. One communications satellite will bring modern education to all seven hundred-plus islands. That alone should be enough to sell it."

"Then why a manned flight? If you want to bring satellite TV to the natives, why not launch from Tanegashima back in Japan?"

"Isn't it a bit late for second thoughts?"

"I'm just passing along the complaints we hear every day."

"Then maybe it's time you started educating your complainers. Satellites are expensive pieces of hardware. Expensive enough for companies like AsiaSat out in Hong Kong to use the shuttle to go up and pluck a broken one out of orbit, have it repaired, and have it launched again. You want to keep a satellite working, you're going to have to send people up to kick the tires every now and again."

"Why not have NASA or the Russians do it?"

"Russia has one foot in the grave, and the shuttle is booked solid for the next decade," sighed Isao. "Besides, they're falling apart. Only a matter of time before another one goes boom. But if we had our own manned space program—just think of it!" Isao thrust a finger toward the OECF man's nose. "The possibilities would be endless! He who rules space rules the world!"

"So that's why we're really here."

"You work for the government. You of all people should know the importance of a good bait and switch."

"Mr. Nasuda," began the OECF man, frowning, "I have an official notice from the Department of Economic Planning. I don't think you're going to like what you see—it's an ultimatum."

[ACT 2]

IN THE CONTROL room, amid the throng of engineers, the traditional prelaunch betting pool was getting underway.

"Ten dollars says it fails," declared Satsuki Asahikawa, the chief medical officer. She was clothed head to toe in crisp white.

"That's pretty harsh, Satsuki," Hiroyuki Mukai grumbled. "How 'bout a little faith, eh?" Fresh from an all-nighter, the chief engineer stared at the monitors with bloodshot eyes.

"Oh, I have a *little* faith."

The flight director, Kazuya Kinoshita, a tall man with hair combed straight back, threw a wad of Solomon Islands dollars in Satsuki's cap. "Until the LS-7 booster proves itself, manned spaceflight is a no go. And judging by the mood in the observation room, the whole show's riding on this one. That said...ten dollars on a failure."

"The whole show? You think they'd cancel the program?"

"Sure do."

"That wouldn't be all bad," interjected Haruyuki Yasukawa, "as long as I could go back to Hamamatsu. I come out here to be a big shot astronaut, and my ride keeps exploding. Now all I have to look forward to are daily torture sessions with Satsuki. I'm not sure how much more I can take."

"That's not torture, it's training."

"That what they're calling it now?"

"You sure you want to go there?"

"There's that look again—like you're sizing up a guinea pig."

"Oh, please."

"You think I didn't notice, Satsuki?"

"Notice what?"

"The last time you had me in the centrifuge, you bumped it up to 20 G, remember?" At 20 G, Yasukawa weighed about one and a half tons—enough load to kill the average person.

"What about it?"

"Before I passed out, you grinned."

"Note to self," she said after a brief pause. "Even air force pilots experience visual distortion at 20 G."

"I know what I saw!"

"Next time we'll just have to try twenty-five," Satsuki purred.

"Says you!"

Two years earlier, before coming to the islands, Yasukawa had been a test pilot in the Japan Air Self-Defense Force. He was stationed in Hamamatsu where he flew experimental Control-Configured Vehicles, or CCVs. All that changed when his commanding officer called him in and asked if he wanted to be an astronaut.

The Solomon Space Association was a new program continuing the work of the former National Space Development Agency of Japan and the Institute of Space and Astronautical Science, and they were about to begin manned-flight operations. The SSA was a local endeavor, operating solely within Solomon Islands territory, or so went the official line. In reality, it was financed with Japanese cash and staffed almost exclusively by Japanese nationals.

Since members of the Japan Self-Defense Force are not generally allowed to serve overseas, Yasukawa had to be temporarily discharged from the service before he could work for the SSA. There would be risks, he knew, but they were risks he was willing to take for a once-in-a-lifetime chance.

"If this launch fails, I'm going back to Hamamatsu."

"If they'll still have you."

"Yeah—what?"

"It's time," interrupted the flight director without looking up from his screen. He flicked on his mike. "T-minus ten minutes. All personnel clear the launchpad!"

[ACT 3]

TEN KILOMETERS AWAY, the voice from the loudspeaker reached a small village in the jungle. The village stood on the slopes of one of the Shiribas, a line of jagged peaks that crossed the island from northwest to southeast. A handful of huts and towers stood around a crude square at the village center.

Each of the huts had a log frame and banana-leaf roof. The floors were raised a full meter off the ground to distance them from the scorpions, snakes, and poisonous ants that teemed on the jungle floor. Walking around barefoot was one thing, but even the locals, who called themselves the Taliho, slept better with a good meter of open air between them and the local fauna. The floor of the chief's hut extended past its walls, forming a balcony that encircled the structure. Baskets and water jugs lined the balcony atop a rug of woven coconut fibers.

The chief sat on the rug with one of his many daughters, Matsuri. Her sharp ears had no difficulty picking out the announcement against the backdrop of birdsong and screeching beasts.

"T-minus ten," she announced to her father.

"Ten minutes until the fireworks."

"We will see them from here?"

"Probably."

"Woo!" Her face glowing, Matsuri rose and leapt from the balcony. A grass skirt and woven bikini top were all that covered her sun-bronzed skin. She was much lighter than the dark-skinned Melanesians, and her chest-length hair fell straight. The Melanesians wore their hair short and kinked.

Matsuri beat the large talking drum at the center of the village, calling her friends to gather. "Fireworks soon! Fireworks soon!"

People streamed from the fields and dense jungle surrounding the village square. Most of the adults were dark-skinned locals, but many of the children had skin the same lighter color as Matsuri's. Everyone wore grass skirts and ornaments made from shells or animal fangs, and little else.

A ripple of excitement passed through the crowd.

"The fireworks are starting! Hurry up!"

"The Japanese are shooting their fireworks."

"It's been a while since the last one."

"Think this one will go high?"

"Last time was all smoke, no fire."

"I hope there's a big fireball this time."

Their chief had explained that the Japanese used fireworks to put things up in the sky. Sometimes the fireworks flew so high they could no longer see them, but more often they burst into balls of flame—much to the villagers' delight.

The adults watched from the square while the children perched in the towers like so many bells. They watched and waited.

Without warning, a pillar of white smoke rose beyond the trees. An orange flame burned at the head of the column, topped by a small silver cylinder. Then came a roar like thunder, sending birds flying from the trees. The silver cylinder sped skyward with incredible power, followed after a forty-five-second delay by the terrible roar of its ascent.

"Go! Go! Go!" the villagers cheered with delight. They clapped their hands; they stomped the ground; they beat on drums and sticks of bamboo.

"C'mon, fireball!"

"Boom! Go boom!"

Bright red flames enveloped the cylinder.

For a moment, a flash as bright as the sun lit the sky, then faded to reveal bits of metal trailing white smoke, scattering like strips of paper in a ticker tape parade.

"Wow!"

"They did it!"

"That was the best one yet!"

Shouts of exultation rose throughout the village.

The chief called down from his balcony. "No work! Today, we feast! We have drink and wild boar! So light the bonfire, and make it big!"

The villagers cheered.

[ACT 4]

THE DRUM OF rain against the ship subsided, and Yukari stepped out on deck. The storm clouds that had brought the squall were already receding into the distance, leaving behind a clear blue sky. The sea air was heavy with the smell of trees and people. Maltide was close.

Maltide was an island covered with dense jungle. Coral reefs and palm trees hemmed the beaches, but the interior was filled with sharp peaks, the occasional black spire breaking through the foliage.

The island was bigger than Yukari had expected. Back in March her uncle had told her of a Japanese enclave on a small island in the Solomons. He had been in Guadalcanal visiting a skipjack tuna cannery for the food-service company he worked for, which was where he had heard the rumors.

Japanese in the Solomons...

Did it mean what she thought it did? She had to find out. Even if it only ended in disappointment.

Unfortunately, there weren't any direct flights between Japan and the Solomon Islands, and getting there using a prepackaged tour would be too expensive. The high school Yukari had been accepted to last spring didn't allow its students to hold part-time jobs, so saving up was out of the question. After brooding over the problem for a few days, she decided to take it to her mother.

"I don't know what good it will do," her mother began. "But who knows? A trip like this on your own—it might be good for you." And like that, her mother handed her five hundred thousand yen in cash.

Yukari's mother was in architectural design, so she made considerably more than the average salaryman. Better still, she wasn't stingy with it. The air of indifference with which she had given Yukari the money was simply intended to annoy her daughter, which it did.

By the time summer vacation rolled around, Yukari was armed with passport, visa, and traveler's checks. She left Narita Airport on July 21 aboard an Air France DC-10 that took her as far as New Caledonia. From there a Solomon Airlines Boeing 737 brought her to Guadalcanal. After a night in a hotel in Honiara, she boarded a ferry. Now she was eight hundred kilometers south of the equator, a world of sun, coral, and jungle.

As the ferry pulled up to the pier, Yukari shouldered a backpack over her windbreaker and pulled on a short-brimmed straw hat she had picked up in Honiara. She stepped off the boat, followed by a stream of men with blackened arms and necks. The rickety wooden pier she found herself on looked as though it might give way at any moment, but after a few heart-stopping steps, she had reached the shore.

A short walk along a road made of crushed oyster shells and

bits of coral brought her to Main Street in the town of Santiago. According to her guidebook, Santiago was the closest thing to a proper city on the entire island. Even so, she couldn't spot a single building taller than the palm trees. A stone mansion from the days of British rule caught her eye. She peered past the outer wall and saw that the grounds had been converted to a marketplace. Stalls led up to the open hall on the first floor of the house, and smoke from grilling fish filled the air. Shoppers carrying baskets and bags of woven hemp filled the market, the pale East Asians standing out against the dark-skinned Melanesians. English was supposed to be the common language here, but what strange, clipped syllables Yukari could make out didn't sound like any dialect of English she'd ever heard. A stucco church stood beside the market, and beyond that stretched rows of small shops.

Yukari was on a missing-person search, so she figured the city hall or the police station would be good places to start. She began exploring the city and before long came across a peculiar street market. A riot of primary colors—reds, yellows, greens—filled her view. At the head of the street stood a brightly colored gate decorated with two dragons.

"I guess anywhere you go, they have a Chinatown."

Amused, she stepped through the gate.

She had scarcely crossed the threshold when someone called to her in accented Japanese. "Miss! Miss! You come from Japan?"

An aging Asian man with ruddy cheeks stood in front of the shop on her left, beckoning her closer. The sign behind him read TIANJIN RESTAURANT in large Chinese characters. Scrawled messily to one side, an addendum in Japanese read RICE PORRIDGE, DIM SUM. JAPANESE WELCOME. STAFF SPEAK JAPANESE.

A stroke of luck. Yukari could hold a light conversation in English, but the pidgin they spoke on the islands was another beast. More importantly, she might overhear something to aid her search in a restaurant that catered to Japanese.

"Hello."

"Hello! You pretty girl! You come inside, you eat. My name is Tianjin Cheung. This my restaurant. Japanese love my food." Mr. Cheung led her inside, peppering Yukari with pleasantries all the while. The shop was decorated with openwork folding screens, black tables and chairs, and all the usual fixtures. A stereotypical Chinese restaurant.

Mr. Cheung brought her a menu with Japanese translations beside each item.

Yukari glanced down the menu. "Um…rice porridge, please."

"Rice porridge? Nothing else? You should eat. Too thin. Bad luck being thin."

Yukari didn't appreciate the pressure tactics but decided she stood more to gain by befriending the proprietor than by getting on his bad side. "Okay, throw in some dumplings."

"Dumplings. Very good. One minute, please."

Mr. Cheung disappeared into the back and returned a moment later carrying a tray laden with a bowl of rice porridge that looked exactly like the paste kids use in arts and crafts, a small bamboo basket of dumplings, and a mystery deep-fried morsel that loosely resembled a twisted doughnut.

He poured Yukari a glass of oolong tea. "You come visit base?"

"Base?"

"Sure, rocket base. Other side of mountain."

"There's a rocket base here? Really?"

"Oh yes. I never tell lie."

"There wouldn't be any Japanese on this base, would there?"

"Oh yes. Only Japanese."

"For real?" Yukari sprang to her feet. Jackpot.

"For real. I never tell lie."

"How do you get there? Is there a train? A bus?"

Mr. Cheung only shook his head.

[ACT 5]

THIRTY MINUTES AFTER the explosion the management team had already been called into a meeting. It was unusual to meet before the initial telemetry analysis was even complete. Whatever this was about, it wasn't going to be good.

Once everyone had settled into their seats, Director Nasuda addressed the team.

"The LS-7 booster that just exploded so fantastically was to be our ticket to manned spaceflight...had it been successful." He cleared his throat before continuing. "These six failures have given us a lot of valuable data. With another year, we'd have ourselves a world-class rocket. But that's another year we don't have." He glared at the assembled managers. "The suits bankrolling this operation, the Department of Economic Planning, have shortsightedly concluded that if this launch failed, our base here in the Solomons would be closed, and the manned spaceflight program would be indefinitely shelved."

Gasps filled the room. This was hardly a revelation, but that did nothing to lessen the shock. "Hamamatsu, here I come," mumbled Yasukawa.

"Not so fast, Yasukawa!" the director barked. "We're not finished yet. If we can get you in orbit in the next six months, they wouldn't dare pull our funding."

"We can't get the LS-7 up and running that soon," said Kinoshita, the flight director. "The first stage is still too unreliable. We need a 99.99 percent safety margin before we go strapping people on top."

"We won't be using the LS-7," Nasuda said. "We're using the

LS-5. What she lacks in lift, she makes up for in reliability."

"Won't work," said Mukai, the chief engineer. "The whole reason we're developing the LS-7 is because the LS-5 doesn't have enough lift."

"Then we reduce the payload. Strip down every system that's not absolutely essential. Shave the critical load coefficient down to 1.05."

Mukai's brow furrowed. "You think that will get us to 99.99 percent?"

"The numbers will work themselves out. If we can just keep that first stage from exploding, we can sail right into low earth orbit."

"I'll do what I can, but I'm not making any promises."

"Fair enough," agreed Nasuda. "Satsuki?"

"Sir?"

"How light can you get Yasukawa here?" Clearly, Nasuda was going to go after every last gram.

"Let's see...He's 170 centimeters tall, and there's not much we can do about his bone mass. I'd say fifty kilograms."

"Do it."

"Yes, sir."

There was a loud bang from the back of the room. The door stood half open, the sound of running footsteps echoing from the hall.

"Yasukawa." Nasuda sighed as he reached for the intercom on the wall. "You there, Kurosu? Yasukawa may be trying to leave the base. See that he doesn't."

[ACT 6]

"MAYBE THAT OLD Chinese guy was right," muttered Yukari. "I should've waited until dark."

There weren't any trains or buses from Santiago to the base on the northeast shore of the island—the base needed to be some-where isolated. A single road, barely wide enough for one truck, wound its way through the mountains from Santiago to the base. Rocket Road. On foot, the going wasn't easy.

Mr. Cheung had suggested that Yukari wait until the evening when the people at the base came to town for dinner. Then she could simply catch a ride with someone on their way back. But Yukari had consulted a map in the restaurant, and the base was only fifteen kilometers away. She figured it would be a three-hour hike at most. She weighed her options after leaving the restaurant and finally decided to hoof it. Now she was regretting that decision.

Rocket Road straddled the Shiriba Mountains, which rose as high as thirteen hundred meters above sea level. The road thread-ed its way through the valleys, making the journey much longer than it appeared on the map. At times the path was steep enough to give a double black diamond ski slope a run for its money.

Yukari had pushed ahead, but youthful exuberance had given way to exhaustion before she had traveled even a third of the distance to the base. Even standing still, she could feel the midday sun beating down on her, sapping her strength and wringing every drop of water out of her. At times the jungle canopy made a tunnel that afforded some protection against the sun, but after spying a python in the branches of a tree, Yukari was disinclined to linger in the shade.

Yukari found a large stone in a small clearing at the side of the road and sat down. She wasn't sure she had the energy to turn back and make it to town, much less press on to the base. Tired and alone, Yukari was on the brink of despair when she heard the sound of an engine approaching.

"Yes! A car!" Yukari bounded off the rock. She walked to the middle of the road, planted her feet, and waited.

The noise suddenly grew louder. A huge car came speeding out of the shadows at the far side of the clearing. It was a Humvee. The driver slammed on the brakes, bringing the car skidding to a stop in front of Yukari.

"Trying to get yourself killed?!" the driver shouted in Japanese. A large man who looked to be in his twenties sat alone in the car. He didn't look happy.

Yukari ran up to the driver-side window. "Could you give me a lift?"

"Outta my way, kid, I'm in a hurry."

"I was heading to the base, but I don't think I can make it."

He unlocked the passenger door. "Time's a-wastin'."

Yukari climbed in. From the outside, the Humvee looked like a Jeep with a roof, but inside it was spacious, big enough to seat four across a single seat. "Better buckle up. It can get a little bumpy."

"Right."

The man slammed his beast of a vehicle into gear, and they sprang forward. Yukari sank into the hard seat as the car jostled her every which way.

She glanced over in the driver's direction. "So..."

"Yeah?"

"You going to Santiago?"

"Hamamatsu."

"What?"

"Hamamatsu. That's *home*."

What was up with this guy?

The Humvee sped through the jungle at terrific speed, brushing past plants that encroached too close on either side. Over the whine of the engine, Yukari made out a low, methodic whir coming from behind and a little above them as well. Whatever it was, it was getting closer.

"Damn, that was fast."

"What's that sound?"

"HSS-2. Security chopper. But they have to catch me first!" he said, upshifting the double clutch and slamming the accelerator to the floor.

The roar of the helicopter blades was almost deafening. A shadow crept over the hood of the Humvee. Overhead a large boat-shaped object seemed to hover. A voice rang out over a loudspeaker, drowning out even the sound of the blades. "Pull over now, Yasukawa, and we can still keep this civil!"

Yukari cast a sideways glance at the driver's seat. Apparently his name was Yasukawa.

"I'm not stopping till I'm back in Hamamatsu!"

"You've got to the count of three before we open up with our Baby Mark II. One!"

Yasukawa's foot didn't move from the pedal.

The Humvee climbed a steep grade, going airborne as it topped the rise.

"Two! This isn't some slack-spined Self-Defense crew you're dealing with. We *will* fire, Yasukawa!"

"Do me a favor!" barked Yasukawa.

"Who, me?!"

"Wave your hands so the chopper can see you."

"But they said they were going to shoot—"

"If you don't want that to happen, better start wavin'."

Yukari leaned out the passenger-side window. The helicopter was trailing them at a distance of about fifty meters. A man leaned out an open side door, pointing something with a long, slender barrel at them.

Yukari waved her arms like mad.

Yasukawa flipped a switch to turn on the Humvee's bullhorn and shouted into the mike. "See this kid, Kurosu? You want her blood on your hands, be my guest!"

The barrel belched flame.

Yukari ducked back inside the car with a yelp.

Something whizzed past her head, exploding where it struck the road in front of them. The Humvee leapt through the rising flames like a lion at the circus.

"You said they wouldn't shoot!"

Rocket fuel burned on the hood of the car. Yasukawa kept driving. "Kurosu doesn't want me to make it to town."

"Kurosu?"

"Chief of security—damn!"

FWOOMP!

The second shell exploded ahead of them, bringing a large gum tree down across the road. Yasukawa jerked the wheel hard to the right, sending the Humvee into the jungle.

"Out!"

Yukari pushed the door open and slid to the ground.

"This way! Run!"

Yukari hurried down a steep trail after Yasukawa. "Why do *I* have to run?"

"If Kurosu catches you, he'll use you as a hostage."

"What? That's psycho!"

"That's island fever."

"Island fever?"

"Far as he's concerned, what happens on the island stays on the island. This whole damn place is a loony bin!"

Yukari kept running. Soon they were out of the jungle and in a familiar sweet potato field. They could see Santiago on the far side.

The helicopter had gained some altitude now, but it didn't show any signs of breaking off the chase.

"He wouldn't dare shoot at us in town," said Yasukawa, jogging across the field.

"But they're watching us."

"We'll lose ourselves in a crowd. Next stop, Chinatown."

"Then what?"

"Shut up and move."

Soon they were in the backstreets of Chinatown. They ducked low, keeping close to the walls of the houses. After darting in and out of what seemed like the hundredth alleyway, Yasukawa walked up to the back of a house and rapped on the door.

"Yo, Cheung! It's me, Yasukawa! Open up!"

The door swung open.

"Look here! Mr. Yasukawa and young lady. What's wrong?"

"Let us in. I'll explain later."

"Okay, okay."

Mr. Cheung stepped aside to let them in. They were in the kitchen at the back of the restaurant.

"Got any empty rooms?"

"*Aiyaa*..." Cheung sighed. Then, with a wink, "You not waste any time. This way, please."

They climbed a flight of stairs up to a small twin bedroom. Apparently the second floor of the Tianjin Restaurant was a hotel.

"Enjoy yourselves. You want something to drink?"

"You got the wrong idea, Mr. Cheung. We're on the lam."

"On the lam?"

Yasukawa produced a one hundred Solomon Islands dollar bill from his pocket and pushed it into Cheung's hand.

"If anybody from the base comes poking around, we're not here."

"Ah, I see. I will keep you on the lam, Mr. Yasukawa," Cheung said with a wink.

"One more thing. I need you to get a boat down to Clepp Point for me. Something that'll get me to Santa Isabel."

"Leave everything to me. You rest here until tonight. I bring you tea."

Cheung soon returned with a small teapot and two cups. Yukari and Yasukawa sat down side by side on the bed. One sip of hot oolong tea and Yukari was already feeling more like herself.

"So, Mr. Yasukawa."

"That's me."

"Feel like explaining why people were shooting missiles at us in the jungle?"

"Yeah, that. Long story short, working conditions on the base took a sudden turn for the worse. I submitted my resignation, but something tells me they didn't accept."

"So that's what that was about?"

"More or less."

Yukari knitted her brow. She poured some more tea into her cup and moved casually to the edge of the bed.

"What's your story? Don't get many girls running around by themselves out here in the middle of nowhere."

Yukari had her doubts about Yasukawa, but if he worked on the base, she decided he was worth the risk. She took a photograph from a pouch on her backpack, a picture of a man and woman posed in front of the ocean.

"Do you know this man?"

The man in the picture was about thirty, handsome, with the look of an eager salesman.

"Nope. Never seen him."

"It's from sixteen years ago, so he'd look a little older now."

Yasukawa took another look. "Sorry, I don't think so."

"Oh..." Yukari's shoulders sank.

"Who is he?"

"My dad."

"You came all the way out here looking for Daddy?"

"I heard there were a bunch of Japanese in the Solomon Islands. I thought maybe he was one of them."

"There are about three hundred at the base, but it's only been there three years."

"What?"

"Only showed up two years ago myself. Sixteen years ago, there wouldn't have been anything to find."

"My dad disappeared before I was born. On my parents' honeymoon."

"Just like that? Gone?"

"Yeah. They were in their hotel—it was their first night on Guadalcanal. He said he was going out to look at the moon, and he never came back."

"I've heard stranger things. Guess that makes you the honeymoon baby."

Silence fell over the room.

"Musta been hard on your mother."

"She said she was all right. She went to the police, and they looked for my dad for a week without finding anything. Then she canceled the rest of her vacation and flew back to Japan. She had a career of her own, so money was never a problem. And I never knew him, so it's not like I miss him. But still…"

The memories came rushing back.

Parents' Day at school.

The class report on *The Return*, a movie about a missing father who suddenly comes home after twelve years.

Ever since elementary school, Japanese class had been one nightmare after another. Teachers really had a thing for assigning essays about your family. Not that the essays themselves were all that bad. The worst part was her classmates. A ring of sympathetic friends would encircle her, and without fail a boy would come to tease her. Then more girls would come to defend her, and before long things were out of hand. When the dust settled, half the class would be looking at her with pity.

Yukari never felt sorry for herself. It was always well-meaning third parties who did it for her. It took a lot of self-control to keep from breaking down sometimes. Yukari was tougher than most, but not that tough.

"The not knowing is the hard part. Was it a random accident? Did he get cold feet and just leave? Did he kill himself? I have to know."

They heard the sound of footsteps on the stairs. The door swung open, revealing the friendly proprietor.

"You have visitors, Mr. Yasukawa."

"Visitors? Who the hell—" A man in combat fatigues entered after Cheung. His eyes were hidden behind sunglasses, and he carried a pistol at his hip. "Kurosu?" Behind him, a bulky man in his fifties pushed into the room. Director Nasuda. The third and final person through the door was a woman in her late twenties with long hair, dressed all in white. "Et tu, Satsuki?"

Yasukawa turned on Mr. Cheung. "You sold me out!"

"Base good for business. Everybody get along, business stay good."

"You just lost a customer."

"Give it up, Yasukawa," said Kurosu. "You're not gettin' off that easy."

"That's right," added Satsuki. "We've got two years of training tied up in you. We can't let you just walk away." She turned to Director Nasuda for agreement, but his attention was squarely on Yukari. Not to be outdone, Yukari held his gaze.

"Who's the girl?" the director asked.

"Leave her out of this! She's just some kid looking for her dad."

"Is that right? Interesting..." he mumbled with disinterest. "Stand up, would you?"

"What? Why?"

"Come on, give us a twirl. Let's have a look at you."

"I asked *why*."

"Humor me!"

Yukari shrugged, then rose from the bed and did a quick spin.

"Satsuki," the director lowered his voice, "how much would you say she weighs?"

Satsuki's eyes flashed. "Somewhere in the neighborhood of thirty-seven kilograms."

"Thirty-seven? Good, good. Measurements?"

"Height, about 154 centimeters, eighty-one centimeters through the chest, fifty-four at the waist, maybe eighty-two at the hips."

She smiled. "The very picture of health."

His eyes still glued to Yukari, Director Nasuda nodded. He mumbled something under his breath.

Yasukawa shouted, "You can't be serious!"

"You stay out of this! We don't have room in our organization for cowards who turn tail and run when they're needed most. You're fired! Go back to Hamamatsu!"

"Wait—what?"

Ignoring him, the director approached Yukari, his voice smooth as silk. "What's your name?"

"Yukari Morita."

"Here looking for your father, was it?"

"That's right."

"There are over seven hundred islands in the Solomons, and every one a jungle. How exactly did you plan on finding him?"

"I, uh..." Before she left, Yukari had just assumed she'd figure things out as she went. It wasn't until she'd reached the islands that she realized how naive she'd been.

"What would you say if I told you we'd help you look for your father?"

"Why would you do that?"

"My name is Isao Nasuda. I'm the director of the space center here on the island. We have helicopters, trucks, ships—even contacts with the local police. Japanese don't exactly blend in on the Solomons. If he's here, we'll find him."

"Really? You'd do that?" Yukari practically leapt up with joy.

"Don't listen to him!" shouted Yasukawa.

The director turned to Cheung. "Take Mr. Yasukawa downstairs and give him something to eat, would you? He gets so excitable on an empty stomach." Then, to Kurosu, "Go with him. We wouldn't want him to have any trouble finding his table."

"On it," replied Kurosu, placing an arm around Yasukawa.

"Hey, let go of me!"

"I give you something very tasty, I promise."

When the three of them had left, Director Nasuda turned back to Yukari. "Sorry about that. Now, where were we? Ah yes, your father. We're prepared to help you look for him. In return, there's something we'd like you to help us with. Call it a...part-time job."

"What kind of job?"

"The lodgings on the base are fully air-conditioned. We have a cafeteria. And we'll pay you, of course."

"What do I have to do?"

"You just need to sit in front of a computer. When a message comes in, you answer. Maybe press a few buttons. So simple a monkey could do it."

It sounded good. Too good to be true, really, but Yukari was prepared to take some chances if it meant finding her father.

"Well, okay. But only if you show me how to do everything."

"Of course," the director beamed. "This is Satsuki Asahikawa. She'll teach you everything you need to know. Isn't that right, Satsuki?"

"Absolutely. If you have any questions, anything at all, just ask." Satsuki smiled from ear to ear, but her eyes were cold as ice. The perfect, unsuspecting guinea pig had fallen right into her lap.

CHAPTER II

SO EASY A MONKEY COULD DO IT

[ACT 1]

YUKARI FOLLOWED SATSUKI ASAHIKAWA down a nondescript corridor. Long hair spilled down her back, and she wore an ultrashort miniskirt and white lab coat with an unlikely pair of red high heels—a somewhat more provocative ensemble than your average physician might wear.

This so-called doctor had spent the last day examining Yukari from head to toe, using every implement imaginable to test the limits of Yukari's body. Satsuki told her she wouldn't be eligible for the job if she didn't pass the tests, so Yukari endured in silence. Throughout the exam, Satsuki's lips remained frozen in a ruby smile. When Yukari asked the results of a given test, she only scribbled notes on a clipboard and said, "Later."

The last test ended at eight o'clock that night.

"Come with me," Satsuki said.

Later was finally here.

Yukari and Satsuki stood inside Director Nasuda's office. A large steel desk piled high with books and papers sat at the center of the room. Nasuda peered at them from behind the bulwark. "How'd it go?"

Satsuki gave a thumbs-up.

"Fit for duty then! Good." Nasuda rose to his feet and walked over to Yukari. "Congratulations," he said, clapping her on the shoulder and giving her a hearty shake. "I knew you had it in you!"

Yukari didn't know what to say. She felt a knot growing in her stomach. The director seemed a little *too* enthusiastic over a part-time job.

"What a day," he continued. "The world's youngest astronaut is born!"

Yukari cocked her head. "Huh?"

Satsuki ignored her. "The perfect payload. High performance, compact, and lightweight."

"All the best Japanese products are," said Nasuda with a nod.

"Um..." Yukari chewed her lip. "Could you say that again?"

"The part about Japanese products?"

"Before that."

"High performance, compact, and lightweight?"

"Before that."

"World's youngest astronaut?"

"That's the one." She swallowed. "You didn't mean...me, did you?"

"Of course! Who else?"

Yukari's jaw hit the floor. "I'm an astronaut?"

"The Solomon Space Association's very own."

Yukari frowned. "I thought all I had to do was sit in front of a machine pushing buttons and answering calls. You said even a monkey could do it."

"They can. They have." Director Nasuda spread his hands. "When you boil it down, what else does an astronaut do, really?"

Only the finest candidates were chosen to be astronauts—the

best of the best, national heroes, the stuff of kids' dreams. The recruiting process didn't take place in a makeshift hotel room on the second floor of a Chinese restaurant. Or at least it wasn't supposed to.

"The Americans, the Russians—they treat their astronauts like heroes, but don't let that fool you. It's all for show, a way to con taxpayers out of their hard-earned dollars," Nasuda added reassuringly. "The computers fly the spacecraft. All the astronaut has to do is sit back and look out the window."

"So why me?"

Satsuki smiled. "You're compact and lightweight."

"Exactly. You see, a rocket is a lot like a pyramid. Every kilogram of astronaut we add at the top takes a whopping seventy kilograms to support at the base." Nasuda gestured at Yukari. "At a mere thirty-seven kilograms, you're not only light, you're small—and that means we can get by with a smaller capsule too. Compared to Yasukawa, the sky's the limit with you."

"Yasukawa—he was an astronaut?"

"*Was.* The thought of losing a little weight scared him. He wanted out."

"What's so scary about going on a diet?"

"You know," Nasuda dismissed her question with a wave. "But we have him to thank for finding you, the SSA's newest—"

"Not so fast," interrupted Yukari.

"Still on the fence? It's perfectly safe, I assure you. Oh, the Americans have lost a shuttle or two, but what do you expect? They can't even make a car that doesn't break down."

"So, this astronaut thing. Will it be over in a month?"

"I figure this first stint should take about half a year."

"But school starts in September."

"You can study here."

"I don't think that will show up on my transcript."

"Hrm. We'll just have to give your mother a call then."

"First things first. If I agree to this, you'll help me, right?"

"Help you what?"

"Find my dad!"

"Oh that. Of course. Not to worry. We'll throw everything we've got at it." Nasuda reached for the phone on his desk. "What's your mother's number?"

Director Nasuda dialed as Yukari rattled off the digits. The Solomon Islands were two hours ahead of Japan; her mother should just be getting home from work.

As the phone rang, the director put it on speaker.

"Hello," Yukari's mother answered.

"Hello, Ms. Morita? My name is Isao Nasuda. I'm the director of the Solomon Space Center."

"The Solomon Space Center? I'm afraid I don't—"

"You have a daughter by the name of Yukari?"

"That's right."

"Our mission here is to put a person into orbit, and as it happens, we're looking for astronauts."

"I don't see what this has to do with us."

"We had the good fortune of meeting your daughter. She's perfect."

"You want Yukari to become an astronaut?"

"We do. Of course she'd need to work here with us for the next six months or so. What do you say?"

"I'm not sure."

"She'll have room and board, naturally. And we'll take care of all her visa paperwork."

"Is Yukari there now?"

"She's right in front of me." The director gestured at the phone. "Go ahead, Yukari. The speaker will pick you up."

"Um, hi, Mom."

"An astronaut? I can't believe what I'm hearing. I think that's worth postponing your search for your father, don't you?"

"They said they'd help me look for Dad if I worked for them."

"Even better."

"You really think it's a good idea?"

"Are you kidding? It's not every day you get the chance to be an astronaut. There's nothing a daughter of mine can't do."

Yukari sighed. That was her mom, all right. "But what about school? You know they won't let us have part-time jobs."

"We'll pull you out for a semester. I'll tell them you're studying abroad."

"So you're totally okay with this?"

"You bet I am. I'm going to be the mother of an astronaut. I like the sound of that."

"Uh, but, the thing of it is—"

"No changing your mind once you start. I won't have any quitters living under my roof."

"Don't worry, I'll stick with it."

"You sound a little sad. Don't tell me you're homesick already."

"No, it's not that."

"I'll come visit as soon as this project settles down, I promise."

"You're not listening to me!"

"Oh, sorry. Just do your best, all right? Say goodbye to the director for me." The phone clicked.

There was a glint in Director Nasuda's eye. "She has a way with words, your mother."

"She's half crazy if you ask me."

"She knows you have the right stuff—why should she stand in your way? So, do we have a deal?"

"I guess."

"Done! We'll make the announcement to the team tomorrow. They'll need to get working on a training schedule for you right away. Things are going to get busy."

"You'll let me know how the search is going?"

"The search?"

"For my dad!"

"Of course, of course. I'll take care of everything."

Yukari took the picture of her parents from her pocket. "His name is Hiroshi Morita. This was taken sixteen years ago—he'd be forty-seven now. He was a computer sales engineer."

Director Nasuda glanced at the photo. "We'll need to make copies for the search team. I'll hang on to this."

"Thank you."

[ACT 2]

THE NEXT MORNING, Satsuki took Yukari to the Fuel Processing Center half a kilometer from the main base. She led her down a hall that smelled faintly of chemicals until they reached a door labeled DEPARTMENT OF MACROMOLECULAR RESEARCH.

Yukari stared in disbelief as Satsuki pointed out the department head, a disheveled woman in a white lab coat and worn tennis shoes with thick glasses that nearly covered her face. She was walking right toward them.

The woman stopped a mere thirty centimeters from Yukari—no doubt the ideal focal length for the glasses. She scanned Yukari, leaning from left to right, trying to find the best angle from which to make whatever observations she was making.

Yukari leaned toward Satsuki. "What's she doing?" she whispered.

"This," said Satsuki, "is Motoko Mihara, head of our chemistry department."

"Take off your clothes." Motoko's voice was coarse and deep.

"Again?" Yukari had been ordered to disrobe half a dozen times the day before. The thought of another day spent slipping in and out of clothes set her teeth on edge. She stared Motoko down as best she could.

Satsuki was all smiles. "Submitting to this sort of examination is part of your job, Yukari."

With a resigned sigh, Yukari got undressed. Again.

"Bend over," ordered Motoko.

Yukari bent over. Without warning, Motoko grabbed her abdomen.

"Hey!"

"Very good. Nice and tight. We shouldn't have any trouble making it." There was genuine delight in her voice.

"I stand behind my product," said Satsuki.

"Trouble making what?"

"Your space suit."

"Space suit? I thought this place was for making rocket fuel."

"Among other things." Satsuki waved an arm around the room. "We can produce almost any chemical you can imagine here. Motoko is a bona fide genius."

"What's that got to do with—Aieee!" Yukari felt something cold and slick on her back.

"Vaseline," said Motoko.

"That would be good to know *before* you start."

"Right. Sorry."

"And *why* are you rubbing Vaseline on my back?"

"We need a mold to cast your suit."

"What for?"

"It has to be skintight."

Genius or not, Motoko's bedside manner needed work.

Satsuki bent down so she was eye to eye with Yukari. "Those NASA astronauts look like someone in a Godzilla costume. Their suits are baggy, loose—you won't be tying shoelaces in one of those, and you can forget about scratching any itches. What's the point of being out in space if you can barely move? Which is why

Motoko developed the skinsuit."

"Skinsuit?"

"Think of it as a second skin. They show up in anime all the time."

"My anime expertise is a little rusty."

"Normally you have to pressurize a space suit with air. It puffs up like a balloon, and even the joints end up stiff."

"Uh-huh."

"With a suit that's skintight, we only need air in the helmet—after all, your skin doesn't have to breathe. So long as the suit can vent sweat and excess heat into space, you're golden. The key is having the right material. Something water permeable, airtight, heat resistant, and flexible while maintaining its shape."

Yukari sighed. "The only part I understood was 'skintight.' Sounds like a pervert's dream."

"Oh, I'm sure you'll have your share of admirers. But don't worry, we'll save the press kit till just before the launch so you're not distracted."

"Maybe some weirdo with a fetish will pay good money for the suit once this is all over."

"I sure hope so—they cost eight million yen each."

Motoko finished covering Yukari in petroleum jelly from the neck down, and with Satsuki's help, they immersed her in fresh plaster, using spatulas to position her so only the back half of her body was submerged.

Motoko leaned over Satsuki. "It takes about thirty minutes to dry. Try not to move."

"Yes, ma'am."

At first the plaster was ice-cold, but after only a few minutes it had become uncomfortably warm.

"Motoko? Is the plaster supposed to get hot?"

"It's a side effect of the congealing process."

"But it keeps getting hotter. You're sure this is normal?"

Motoko watched as sweat beaded on Yukari's forehead. She laughed. "I need you to do something for me, Yukari."

"What's that?"

"Trust me."

[ACT 3]

THAT AFTERNOON, AS Yukari recuperated in the barracks, Director Nasuda was addressing an assembly of the department heads.

"Good news from the Department of Economic Planning. They've agreed to delay cutting the program if we can get a person into space by year-end—and not one day later."

The members of the team glanced nervously at one another. That only gave them four months—extremely tight.

"Now, as for Yukari's training. This isn't Yasukawa we're dealing with—she's never even flown a plane, much less a spacecraft. We've got an uphill battle ahead of us. What are our priorities?"

The flight director, Kinoshita, raised his hand. "Courage, knowledge, familiarity. If she panics during the mission, we've got a problem. She's going to be locked in a cramped capsule, alone, with a hundred tons of explosives under her feet propelling her into space at eight kilometers per second under 8 G of force."

"Put that way, it's enough to scare me."

"We could simply...not mention the risks."

Director Nasuda shook his head. "Out of the question. If all we wanted was a witless stowaway, we might as well launch a monkey. The whole point of a manned program is to send up someone who knows the risks and is willing to face them. Even if that person is a teenage girl."

The room fell silent.

Satsuki cut through it like a knife. "We should start with solo survival training."

"A parachute drop into the jungle?"

"Exactly."

"Some of the tribes on this island aren't exactly friendly. All well and good if she runs into the Taliho, but what about the rest?"

"So we send her in packing heat." Kurosu patted the side-arm at his hip. "If she can get off a warning shot, they'll scatter like roaches."

"You want to ask a teenage girl to jump into a jungle crawl-ing with potentially hostile natives? She'll be on the first plane back to Japan."

"Leave that to me," said Satsuki. "Give me one week. I'll run her through the centrifuge and multi-axis trainer until she doesn't know which way is up."

"And that will work?"

"Absolutely. I'll push her right to the edge. By the time we put her on the helicopter, she'll be so exhausted she won't fear any-thing, even death. She'll do whatever we tell her to."

Kinoshita nodded slowly. "We're going to induce post-traumatic shock."

"Bingo!" Satsuki grinned. "I'm starting to like her. She's healthy, takes orders—she's even cute. I'm curious to see what can be done with her."

"I'll try to have her suit ready by then," said Motoko. "I want to get data on its performance in a tropical environment."

Kinoshita rolled his eyes. "Sometimes you two scare me."

"Then it's settled," declared Nasuda. "Satsuki will begin endur-ance training. Kinoshita will handle her studies. Swamp her with homework."

Director Nasuda turned to Kurosu. "You're going to teach her how to handle firearms. That should tickle your drill-sergeant bone."

"She'll be a Green Beret by the time I'm through with her."

"You have your assignments. Get to work!"

[ACT 4]

THREE DAYS LATER, it was time to begin. Satsuki brought Yukari to the astronaut training facility, a large building next to the command center.

"This," said Satsuki, "is your desk. Not that you'll be seeing much of it."

Yukari's desk was conveniently located in the office of Chief Medical Officer Satsuki Asahikawa.

Satsuki pointed at stacks of neatly folded clothing on the desk. "These are your training clothes. Shorts, T-shirts, jumpsuits, swimwear—the same things we've been using in your tests. You'll also find towels, caps, shoes, tampons, maxis. There's a locker in the dressing room—you can keep all this there. If you run low on anything, put in a requisition with the supply department."

"Okay."

"The rest is your textbooks, notebooks, calculator, and so forth."

"Got it."

"Well, let's get started, shall we? Beginning tomorrow you'll spend time in the pool and gym before breakfast. Part of your endurance training. Today you get to skip that. Let's put you in the centrifuge to work on your G tolerance."

Satsuki escorted Yukari to a circular room in the basement of the training facility. In the middle of the room was an odd-looking piece of machinery with two arms—one short, one long. At the end of the long arm was a cage big enough to hold one person. The other arm ended in a large counterweight to ensure the entire device remained level while spinning.

"This is the centrifuge. You might have seen something like it at an amusement park."

"I rode one at Toshimaen once."

"This is just an industrial version of the same thing. I'll give you instructions over the intercom. Just do what I tell you and you'll be fine."

"All right."

"Go on, hop in the cage. I believe the best way to learn is by doing. Don't worry, I won't push you too hard."

The cage loosely resembled the control room of a construction crane. Yukari opened the door and wriggled in. It was a tight fit. She sat facing the middle of the room, toward the centrifuge's central axis. There was a small window directly in front of her and beneath it a panel with a row of switches. Cables snaked all around her.

Satsuki reached in through the door and fastened Yukari into a sturdy four-point harness. She placed a headset on Yukari's head and attached a series of sensor wires.

"All set. Just sit tight." Satsuki closed the door and walked out of the room.

Light shone through the glass separating the control room. Satsuki appeared behind the glass. "Can you hear me?" Her voice crackled through the headphones.

"Yeah."

"Straighten your back and place your arms on the armrests."

"Okay."

"Here we go. You'll be at 2 G in three seconds."

Brrrrrm.

Yukari felt a dull thud, and then the centrifuge began to move.

"Whoa."

Every vehicle Yukari had ever ridden in had started slow and built up speed. This was different. The acceleration was instantaneous, like pushing a toy car across the room. It didn't follow a curve, it was a straight line—and it was just getting warmed up.

The spinning grew faster. Everything outside the window was a blur. The centrifuge began to creak, and her body sank deep into the seat.

"Okay, 3 G...4 G..." Satsuki's voice was mechanical.

Yukari felt her stomach contorting. And not just her stomach. Her lungs, her intestines, her brain—it felt as though someone had put them in a vise.

"Now 5 G...Any changes on the panel?"

"Th-the second light from the right came on."

"Those are illuminated switches. I want you to push any of them that light up."

"Okay—huh?" She tried to lift her arm, but it remained glued to the armrest. It felt as though it were made of lead.

At 5 G, Yukari's body would weigh five times as much as normal. So if her arm weighed two kilograms, it felt like ten.

"I can't lift my arm."

"This is only 5 G. Just pretend you're trying to lift a bucket of water."

"Easy for you to say."

Her hand trembled as she peeled it off the armrest, but she managed to press the button. The light went off.

As it did, another went on.

"Turn the lights off as quickly as you can."

"Ugh."

Straining under the effort, Yukari used both arms to press the button.

"Good. Let's see how you handle six."

The centrifuge whined.

"Hey!"

"You're on a course to crash. If you don't turn off all the lights within thirty seconds, the centrifuge will automatically accelerate by 1 G."

"Don't I get a say in this?!"

"Afraid not."

Three lights blinked on. It took all of Yukari's strength to reach the first button. As she did, her arm shook as though it were cramping, and she pressed the adjacent button by mistake. It lit up.

Brrrrrm.

She barely managed to turn off a single light within the time limit. The centrifuge accelerated without mercy.

Yukari's bones ground against each other. She grimaced in pain.

"Now 7 G." Satsuki chuckled.

Yukari's face stretched. She sat powerless as the next thirty seconds expired.

"Now 8 G."

Yukari was overcome by a terrible headache. Her vision began to dim, her heart raced, and her breath grew shallow.

"Breathe with your stomach or you'll suffocate."

She wanted to ask how, but the words wouldn't come. Her ribs pressed against her back, crushing her lungs. She couldn't even force air down her throat.

Another thirty seconds passed.

"And 9 G." Satsuki giggled.

A tunnel closed in around her vision. Her breathing was labored. Her heart was beating two hundred times per minute. A haze clouded her thoughts.

The world went black.

[ACT 5]

YUKARI WOKE UP in her bed. Satsuki was with her, the woman's back facing the bed. The last moments before Yukari had passed out came back to her.

"You..."

"You're awake. How do you feel?"

"You tried to kill me."

"Don't be silly. You're alive, aren't you?" Satsuki's face was expressionless.

"You enjoyed that."

"You kept a cool head." Satsuki wrote something on her clipboard.

"Don't try to change the subject. I heard you laughing."

"You were doing so well. The machine kept accelerating, but you didn't pass out. I was happy for you."

"That's not what it sounded like from where I was sitting."

"You must've misunderstood, that's all." Satsuki glanced at her watch. "Oh, look at that. It's time for class. Don't want to be late on your first day."

"Just let me rest a little first."

"No time."

Satsuki dragged her out of bed.

When she reached the classroom, Kazuya Kinoshita was waiting for her. His silver-rimmed glasses sparkled.

"You're late," he barked.

"I blacked out."

"I don't want excuses. An astronaut has to be able to manage her schedule. Next time you're late, I'll keep you for an extra three hours."

Yukari wondered where they found these people. How did someone so young—Kinoshita couldn't have been much past forty—get to be such a hard-ass?

"Now let's try to make an astronaut out of you. Turn to page ninety-two in *The Feynman Lectures on Physics*, Volume I."

Yukari flipped to the page he'd asked her to. It was a monster of a book.

"Orbital mechanics are governed by Kepler's laws. Read them out loud."

"Let's see...Kepler's first law: The orbit of every planet is an ellipse with the sun at one focus."

"Keep going."

"Kepler's second law: A line drawn between the sun and a planet will sweep out equal areas in equal periods of time. Kepler's third law: The squares of the orbital periods of any two planets are proportional to the cubes of the semimajor axes of their orbits."

As she read, Kinoshita had written an equation and several numbers on the board.

"This is the equation for a planet's orbit. Use these initial values and the gravitational constant to integrate the equation."

"Integrate?"

"You don't know integral calculus?" His voice had jumped an octave.

"I don't think we ever learned that."

"Let's try this then." Kinoshita wrote another equation on the board. "You must be able to calculate a binomial expansion."

This new formula looked more familiar. She just needed to plug in the values for the variables.

"So, what's the vector after one second?"

"But those are eight-digit numbers."

"Use your calculator."

"Oh, right." Yukari took out the calculator she'd been given that morning. She flipped on the switch, and froze. "Huh?"

"What's wrong?"

"It doesn't have an equals button."

"Of course it doesn't!" He looked like he might burst a vein.

"Haven't you heard of reverse Polish notation?"

Yukari brought her hand down on her desk with a bang. "Obviously not!"

"Then I'm going to spend the next five minutes drilling it into your head. When I'm finished, you'll never want to touch a normal calculator again."

"Tyrant!"

"What did you call me?"

The next two hours were a nightmare. Dejected and with a mountain of homework in her hands, Yukari walked out of the classroom.

[ACT 6]

THAT AFTERNOON YUKARI started survival training with Toshiyuki Kurosu, the chief of security. Kurosu took one look at her in T-shirt and shorts and thrust a pair of fatigues at her.

"Change into this."

A short ride in a Humvee brought them to a firing range at the foot of the Shiriba Mountains. Dense tropical jungle surrounded them on all sides. There were sandbags everywhere, and the ground was crisscrossed with trenches just wide enough for one person. The entire range was fenced with barbed wire.

Kurosu spoke to Yukari across the hood of the Humvee. "This is the SSC firing range. I intend to spend the next week teaching you how to survive in any environment the tropics can throw at you." Kurosu squinted at her. "Tell me. What's the key to survival?"

"Hmm..."

"Shoot before you are shot!" Kurosu shouted at the top of his lungs.

"Wha—?"

"That is the only way you will survive! The enemy is everywhere. You must kill the enemy without hesitation. If you do not kill the enemy without hesitation, the enemy will kill *you*!"

Yukari stared blankly at Kurosu. Another freak.

He took a large pistol out of a duffel bag. "Forty-five caliber, Colt Government M1911A1. Your new best friend." He held the gun out to Yukari. "Take it."

It felt heavy in her hands, a lifeless mass of metal.

His hand reached into the duffel bag for more loot. "This is your gun belt. Wrap it around your waist. This is a magazine—seven rounds each. Always remember how many rounds you have left. Cleaning kit and tools—you gotta be able to strip and clean your weapon with your eyes closed in the middle of a firefight."

"Question."

"Proceed."

"I thought survival training would be more about pitching tents and scavenging for food."

"Can you kill the enemy with a tent?" Kurosu bellowed. "First order of business is survival. If you can kill a man, you can hunt an animal. Then we'll worry about tents."

"I don't believe this."

"Hmph. If your brain won't get it, your body will. Follow me."

Kurosu led Yukari to a corner of the range and showed her how to handle the gun he'd given her. Slap a fresh magazine in the bottom, pull back the slide, release the safety.

"Squeeze the trigger, kill the enemy. Got it?"

"Yes, sir."

"Show me."

Kurosu pressed a button on a nearby control panel, and a man-shaped target popped up in front of them.

"Aim for the heart. Keep your feet apart, bend your back. Hold the grip with both hands."

Yukari followed each instruction precisely.

"Fire!"

Bang!

A massive jolt ran through Yukari's arms and into her shoulders, shaking her from head to toe. She staggered backward.

"Wrong! Do not close your eyes when discharging your weapon!"

"Do you have anything...smaller?"

"Your weapon must strike fear in the heart of the enemy. One more time. Like you mean it."

Bang!

The recoil knocked her back again. The bullet hadn't even grazed the target.

"Hold the grip good and tight. Squeeze the trigger, real light. Now fire."

Bang!

A hole appeared in the target's stomach.

"I hit it!"

"Empty these." Kurosu set six more magazines on the table.

She fired all forty-nine rounds. When she finished, she couldn't feel anything below her shoulder. But Kurosu was just getting started. He made her change her stance and fire off another forty-two before taking her to an obstacle course covered with track-and-field equipment.

"You will scale that wall, crawl under that barbed wire, and dive into that trench."

Yukari sighed. It sounded like the first level of a video game.

"You will also crouch the entire time because I will be standing here firing at you with a machine gun." Kuroso hefted an M-60. "I will be firing live rounds. If you stand higher than you should, you will be in a world of hurt."

"You're kidding."

"Scared? You should be. It costs a lot of money to train an astronaut," he said. "I'm here to weed out the undesirables. Now suck it up and move!"

"But that's not fair."

"Not fair?"

"You've got a machine gun, and all I have is this pistol. I won't stand a chance."

"Well, well, well." His face split into a grin. "You want to shoot back? Keep me honest?"

"You said shoot or be shot. I want a machine gun too. Something small and light I can run with. One that shoots lots of bullets."

"Aren't you full of surprises. I've got just the thing." Kurosu reached back into his duffel bag and produced a small, angular machine gun. "This is an Ingram MAC-11. She's compact and lightweight, but she still packs a punch."

"Perfect."

"She'll dance when you fire her, so hold on good and tight to the silencer with your left hand."

"No problem. Now all I need are some bullets."

"Help yourself."

Their war games lasted the rest of the day. With bullets whizzing by overhead, Yukari realized it was a lot harder to be an astronaut than she had imagined. But she wasn't going to give up yet.

CHAPTER III

GIRL OF THE JUNGLE

[ACT 1]

A FULL WEEK had passed since Yukari began training. Her body was bruised, her back ached, she had sprains in places she didn't know she could sprain—she was a walking ball of pain. Physically and mentally Yukari was at the breaking point.

Satsuki escorted her to the Fuel Processing Center. Motoko Mihara was waiting for her in the same room where they had taken a cast of her body the previous week.

Motoko pointed proudly to a gleaming white space suit hanging from a rack. "Ta-da! Your skinsuit is finally ready."

Yukari glanced at the suit with disinterest.

The material was ultrathin, a mere two millimeters thick, and it formed one continuous piece, like a wet suit. A double-layered fastening mechanism extended from the neck to the waist. The chest bore the SSA logo, and beneath it ASTRONAUT YUKARI MORITA was neatly printed in ten different languages—in the event she had to make an emergency landing in some remote part of the globe.

"Out of those clothes—underwear, everything," said Motoko.

Yukari stripped without protest. Taking off her clothes on command had become a nonevent. She had been poked and prodded by every instrument known to man. Privacy was not a luxury afforded astronauts.

The space suit was precisely 3 percent smaller than Yukari but had some give. With her arms and legs inside, the material fit snugly against her body—a second skin, just as Satsuki had said. From the neck down, the only part of the suit that wasn't skintight was a device to collect urine in the crotch that resembled an oversized maxi pad. For solid waste, you would just have to hold it.

There were ports in the back that provided power to the heaters embedded in the material of the suit, as well as an array of sensors that monitored body temperature and power flow. A ring around the neck would fasten the helmet to the suit, but the helmet was still in production.

"Try moving around. It might feel a little stiff."

"A bit."

"I designed it for optimal comfort while seated in the capsule, but I think it holds up well enough in general use."

"I guess—my chest could use some support though. You sure I can't wear a bra?"

"Out of the question. Your skin has to be in direct contact with the suit." Motoko thought for a moment. "Maybe if you wore it *out*side the suit."

Yukari frowned.

"I think it looks cute on you," said Satsuki. "A science fiction heroine straight out of an anime."

"I'm curious to see how strong it is in practice, how long it can be continuously worn," said Motoko. "It has a sturdy silicone rubber base, but if it gets scratched up too badly it might tear. Of course, in a vacuum, even if it does break, it won't pop—no air inside."

Yukari was unimpressed.

"Keeping you in it for two or three days should tell me what I need to know. If it gets too uncomfortable, take it off and give your skin some air."

"But try to avoid it," added Satsuki. "This is a test, after all."

"A test? Now?"

"A field test, yes. You'll be camping out."

"But what about class? And endurance training?"

"Those are on hold."

"Woo-hoo!" Yukari's face lit up with joy.

"Come on, we need to get to the landing field."

"Landing field?"

"You heard me." Satsuki smiled.

[ACT 2]

THE HSS-2 HELICOPTER climbed straight into the sky. The sliding door on its side was open, providing Yukari a breathtaking view of the distant island of Malaita and the coral reef that ringed Maltide. The reef glimmered like jade beneath the tropical sun.

Yukari was strapped snugly into a parachute harness, and she wore a gun secured to one shoulder over her new space suit. Kurosu sat beside her.

"Your chute will open on its own. You can guide your descent with the cables on either arm, but you'll probably just make things worse. If you're headed into a tree, tuck in your legs and cover your face with your hands."

"What about my chest? A hit there hurts like hell."

"Your choice then, face or chest. Once you're on the ground, check your weapon first, then examine your surroundings. If you get lost, stay out of the rivers. Try to follow a ridge. Remember your training and you'll do fine."

"The only thing you trained me to do was shoot."

"That's all you need to know. The rest is details."

Yukari had suddenly found herself the sole participant in a survival training mission. She was about to parachute into a jungle, alone, with no radio and only a day's worth of rations.

She followed the orders without a word of protest. Either the team's plan to wear her down with a week of grueling training had succeeded in numbing her to fear, or she had more courage than they had given her credit for.

The helicopter climbed to an altitude of 1,200 meters. The lines of the base, looking uncannily like the geoglyphs at Nazca, receded into the distance. Dense jungle rolled beneath them.

"We're at the drop zone. Get ready."

Yukari unfastened her seat belt and stood at the edge of the door. The wind was ice-cold. A small cloud passed beneath them.

"Now jump!"

Yukari leapt into the air. For a brief moment, she was in free fall—weightless. A hard jolt shook her as the parachute unfurled overhead. It was a paraglider, giving her some lift and forward motion.

The helicopter didn't linger to see that she landed safely.

The ground rose slowly beneath Yukari's dangling feet. Or what seemed slow, at first. Her shadow moved across the canopy of the trees at a brisk pace of better than thirty-five kilometers per hour.

As she drew closer to the ground, the paraglider began to shudder and lurch. Banking sharply to one side, it changed course, descending into a deep valley that lay in shadow.

"Uh-oh…" The side of the valley rose in a steep, green slope. It was coming at her fast.

"Not good."

Yukari fought with the controls, but she couldn't remember how to steer.

"C'mon! Not *that* way!"

Yukari crashed into the jungle canopy. From a distance, lush green foliage looks soft and welcoming.

It isn't.

[ACT 3]

"JUMPED RIGHT OUT, did she?"

Kurosu had been briefing Director Nasuda on the drop. He liked what he was hearing.

"We dropped her over Taliho territory, but there's no guaranteeing that's where she put down," said Kurosu. "Good chance she broke a leg coming in, but these things happen."

"Can't be helped, I suppose."

"She makes it through this, it's smooth sailing from here on out. The kid's a natural. Squeezes a trigger gentle as you please."

"You don't say?"

"Could be her feminine disposition helps her keep a cool head."

"Could be." Nasuda folded his arms. "I admit, she's come further in a week than I would have guessed. I'm starting to think we should bring her aboard permanently."

"Why not? Put one of our boys on, you lose another hundred kilograms of payload. You'd be a fool to send them up if Yukari pans out."

"If. And then there's the problem of not having a backup. I'd rest a lot easier knowing we had at least one more—another girl about the same size."

Nasuda knew the odds of stumbling across another candidate were slim to none. He could always find someone by actively recruiting, but the press would have a field day, and then he would end up defending his decision to an outraged public.

"Good work, Kurosu. Dismissed."

"Sir." Kurosu turned and left the room.

Nasuda sat lost in thought. His eyes came to rest on a photograph on his desk that had collected a thin layer of dust—the photograph of Yukari's father.

"Who goes missing on their honeymoon?"

Nasuda lifted the photograph and examined it.

"Where have I seen him before?" The color left his face. "I don't believe it!"

He had to act quickly. If Yukari found her father, she would have no reason to stay and become an astronaut. Nasuda picked up the phone and started to dial.

[ACT 4]

YUKARI GROANED AND opened her eyes.

She had come to rest on a thick branch. Her entire body throbbed with pain. She tested her arms and legs one by one—nothing seemed to be broken. She was surrounded by trees, trees, and more trees.

Yukari reached for a small branch to pull herself up. *Squish.* Her fingers closed around the body of a snake.

"Aiiieee!" She leapt from the branch without a second thought and came crashing down. Finally on the ground, Yukari nursed a fresh bruise. "I hate the jungle!"

After a short rest, she rose to her feet. She removed the parachute harness and hefted the pack containing her rations and survival kit onto her back. A quick inspection of the handgun holstered on her shoulder revealed no problems. Her space suit had survived in one piece, and although the air was brutally hot, it was nothing Yukari couldn't handle.

She checked her compass to get her bearings. "Looks like I came down on the north side of the ridge." The map showed two or three valleys that seemed similar to the one in which she had landed. If she followed the valley downhill, she should reach the coast. She remembered Kurosu's advice about climbing to the top of a ridge if she got lost.

"I'm not lost yet."

By the time she had decided on a path down the valley, Yukari was already feeling better. This was the most freedom she had had in a while. There wasn't anyone to torture or berate her here.

Yukari drew a deep breath. "Yodel-ay-hee-hoo!"

Her surroundings pressed in around her. Inseparable layers of trees, moss, flowers, and vines. Curtains of milk-white sunlight. Birds and butterflies drifting on the wind. The forest brimmed with life, and yet it seemed to sleep.

"I'm in the middle of the jungle..."

Swallowing her fear, she set out.

[ACT 5]

IT WAS ALMOST noon. Yukari was about to sit down for a delicious MRE lunch when she heard a sound from the bushes on her right. She froze, not even breathing, and listened. Kurosu's words raced through her head. *Shoot or be shot.*

She took her Colt Government from its holster and held it with both hands. She released the safety.

"Wh-who's there?" The words came out in a whisper.

There was no answer.

Yukari stood motionless, muscles taut. She heard the sound again. It was coming from about thirty meters away. Closer than before. Whoever it was might try to flank her, so she had to find out who it was. Gun drawn, she pressed forward.

The bushes in front of her rustled. Yukari nearly jumped out of her skin and her skinsuit.

"Who's there? Don't move!" And then, in her best English, "Freeze!"

"My name is Matsuri."

"Wha—?"

The answer came in Japanese. Or were Yukari's ears playing tricks on her?

The bush rustled once more, and a girl about the same height as Yukari stepped out of the jungle. She had smooth, bronze skin, and her hair was long and straight. She wore nothing but a grass skirt and woven bikini top. What she lacked in clothing the girl made up for in accessories. Animal fangs, seashells, and a bounty of colorful fetishes graced her arms, legs, and neck. Some looked as though they might even be magical talismans.

A long hunting spear rested on the girl's shoulder like a fishing rod, the day's catch hanging from its tip.

"Um, hello?"

"Hi." Matsuri smiled warmly. "I haven't seen you before." Her Japanese had a strange accent, but it was definitely Japanese. She peered at Yukari with wide, black eyes.

"My name's Yukari."

"There are many poisonous snakes this way, Yukari."

This was useful information. "I didn't know." Regaining her composure, Yukari returned her gun to its holster. "You know your way around here?"

"Oh yes." There was pride in her voice.

"I'm trying to get back to the Solomon Space Center. You know where it is?"

"*Hoi*. The fireworks place. It's not far, but you need to go back that way."

"Oh..."

"Come on. I'll show you."

Matsuri started off into the jungle. She moved like a cat, her long legs knowing instinctively where to step. Yukari kept up as best she could.

"Slow down."

"Ah, you are not used to this place."

"You noticed."

"This place can be unforgiving to outsiders. Sometimes the anthropologists come. It is very hard on them."

"Anthropologists?"

"I think that's the word. My Japanese isn't very good. Do you speak English?"

"Yeah, but I'd rather stick with Japanese."

"Yukari is *wantok*." Matsuri grinned. "Our chief says all Japanese are *wantok*."

"What's *wantok*?"

"One talk. *Wantok*. It's pidgin for someone who speaks only one language."

This barefoot girl in the middle of the jungle was bilingual?

"So, Matsuri..."

"*Hoi?*"

"Where did you learn Japanese?"

"Our chief taught me."

"Your chief sounds pretty smart."

"Oh, he is. He knows everything. You want to meet him? It's not far."

"Sure, why not?" If the chief was some sort of Nipponophile, Yukari thought there might be a chance he knew something about her father. As best she could judge from Matsuri, they didn't seem to be headhunters, and if she got in trouble, she still had her gun. "Let's get going."

"Woo!" Matsuri jumped with joy. "Follow me!"

"Hey, wait up!"

Yukari struggled to keep up with Matsuri as she raced through the jungle. They ran for half an hour before emerging in a large clearing. A handful of huts stood on stilts, and there was one tall watchtower. A bonfire crackled happily in the plaza at the center of the village. There was a large talking drum that had been carved out of a tree.

"Wow." Yukari knew they weren't advanced, but she hadn't expected this. It was something out of a fairy tale.

Matsuri cut across the plaza and climbed up into one of the huts. "Dad, I brought somebody to visit."

A voice drifted down. "Speaking Japanese today, are we, Matsuri? And what's this about a visitor?" His Japanese was fluent, almost native.

"Come on up, Yukari." Matsuri waved down from a crude balcony.

"Coming." She clambered up a log ladder and into the hut. There was no door, only a curtain of banana leaves. Inside it was pitch black.

As Yukari's eyes adjusted, the details of the room came into focus. A rug of woven palm fiber and baskets of the same material. Clay pottery. A large, round stone. Decorations made from seashells.

Matsuri sat cross-legged on the floor. Behind her sat a muscular man with a disheveled beard. This was how Yukari imagined cults got started.

"Um, hello. I met Matsuri in the jungle. My name's Yukari Morita."

"That's quite a coincidence." The chief spoke in a soft voice.
"Oh?"

"My name is Morita too. Hiroshi Morita."

Yukari's heart stopped. That was her father's name.

[ACT 6]

YUKARI STARED INTO the man's face. The sun had darkened his skin, and his hair and beard had grown unchecked, but there was no question about it. A shiver ran through her.

"Could I ask you something?"

"Yes?"

"What's your wife's name?"

"Let's see, there's Toto, Onikay, Papayto, Lungia, Cavay." The chief counted off the names on his fingers. "Lebi, Tsupua, Manaen, Walikay, Tongua, Kaua, Faula, Lenikay, Kevanamua, Koina, Lakiki. There are another ten or so, but I can't place their names right now."

"Uh, okay. What about Japan? Did you ever get married there?"

"Japan? Yes, actually. Hiroko, I think her name was."

Whatever doubt had lingered in Yukari's mind, it was gone now. The man in front of her was her father.

"I'm Hiroko Morita's daughter."

"I never knew she remarried."

"She didn't. That first night on the honeymoon? Mission accomplished."

"How about that? Nice of you to come visit your old man."

"Nice of me to come *visit*?" That was the last straw. "Is that the best you can do after walking out on your wife and your daughter?

What are you even doing out here in the middle of a jungle?"

"I'm the chief."

"And?"

"It's a long story."

"So what happened that night in Guadalcanal?"

"I remember it like it was yesterday." The chief stared into the distance. "I was in the hotel with Hiroko—it was our first night there—and I happened to look out the window. The moon was coming up, and it looked so lovely I decided to go for a walk."

"By yourself?"

"Hiroko said she was sleepy. So I went down to the beach alone."

"Then what?"

"The moon was high and bright. The waves shone white in the moonlight. It was like I was walking in a dream world."

"Spare me the poetry."

"I noticed a single canoe on the water, heading straight for where I stood. When it reached me, I got in. We rowed for two days before reaching Maltide."

"Whoa, whoa, whoa. Back up. Why did you get in the canoe in the first place?"

"I'm not sure."

"Not the answer I was looking for."

"The men from the canoe brought me here, to the village. The chief came out and told me they had been waiting for me. He said their shaman had called me to them with the help of the spirits."

"As in magic?"

"A small tribe like the Taliho will die out if they only marry within the tribe. They turn to outsiders like me to bring in new blood."

"So what's with the mumbo jumbo then?"

"I can't really say. That's more of Toto's specialty. Toto is Matsuri's mother—she probably knows more about it than I do."

"Ask away," said Matsuri, smiling.

"How does this magic work?"

"We burn grass in the plaza, and the shaman chants the sacred words. Everyone gathers around to drink and dance the whole night. It's lots of fun."

"That's it." Yukari stood. "Start packing—we're going back to Japan."

"We?" asked the chief.

"Yes, *we*. You can't just leave your family and run off to party on some tropical island."

"I wouldn't call it partying. I'm the chief here. I negotiate with other tribes. I even wage war, when it comes to it."

"What about making up for your past? I grew up without a father because of you! And you wouldn't believe what I've been through on this island looking for you."

"I was wondering about the clothes. It says you're an astronaut with the Solomon Space Association."

"Long story. Basically, I took this part-time job as an astronaut to try and find *you*."

"Good work, if you can get it."

"Hardly. The last week of my life has been a living hell. But that's over now. We're going home to Japan, and you're going to apologize to Mom."

"You can't do that." The warmth in his voice was gone now.

"Do what?"

"Quit your job. People are counting on you. It would be irresponsible."

"Irresponsible? You left your wife on your honeymoon!"

"That has nothing to do with you."

"Oh yeah?"

"I was a computer sales engineer. I know the impact it can have on a team when someone pulls out. Take that space suit, for example—obviously custom-made. It probably cost millions of yen. And the rocket is in another league entirely."

"You're not talking your way out of this." Yukari drew her Colt.

"If you don't come back to Japan with me, I'll shoot you."

"Easy, Yukari." The chief motioned for her to be calm. "Think about what you're doing here."

"I know exactly what I'm doing."

"I don't think you do." A smile flashed across the chief's face. "You want me to come home with you, right?"

"Yeah."

"You want a normal, happy family, right?"

"That's the idea."

"And you expect that to happen at gunpoint?"

"Well, uh..."

"I'll make you a deal. If you see this astronaut job through, I'll come back with you to face the music in Japan. I'll throw myself at Hiroko's feet and beg forgiveness." There was still doubt in Yukari's eyes. "Look, there are over three hundred Taliho here, and I'm responsible for them. I can't just get up and leave. While you're finishing your job, it will give me time to make arrangements for someone to replace me."

"I don't know."

"And what about your mother? Does she even want me to come back?"

"I think so."

"Did she tell you that?"

"Not exactly," Yukari admitted.

"I didn't think so. So there's no need to rush things. What do you say?"

"When my astronaut job is done, you'll come back to Japan? You promise?"

"I promise."

"You'll have to clean yourself up. Get a job, help Mom with the bills."

"Naturally."

"And you have to get me and Mom presents on our birthdays."

"Gladly."

"Remember, you promised."

"Cross my heart and hope to die."

"Break that promise and you just might."

Yukari returned her gun to its holster.

The chief stretched. "It's been a while since I had a nice long conversation like that. Really works up the appetite." His eyes moved to the animals Matsuri had brought back from her hunt. "What say we roast up some grub?"

"Okay." Matsuri stood up with her catch and turned to Yukari. "You should stay and eat with us, Sis."

[ACT 7]

YUKARI AND A group of villagers sat in a circle around the bonfire. Matsuri turned the mystery meat roasting on the spit as juices began to drip down into the fire. "All done," she said.

Yukari sat on a flat stone, watching Matsuri—her half sister. The chief had a couple dozen wives, which meant Yukari probably had dozens of half brothers and sisters in the village. But Matsuri was special.

Aside from Yukari herself, Matsuri was the chief's oldest child. They didn't keep precise records, but she had been born only one or two months after Yukari. They were practically the same age.

"Looks good, doesn't it, Yukari?" Matsuri took a slice of meat from the shoulder and handed it to her.

"Yeah, I'm starved—Ow! It's hot!"

Yukari continued to study Matsuri as she chewed the strange-smelling meat. She was interested in more than her age.

"*Hoi?* What is it, Yukari?"

"How much do you weigh, Matsuri?"

"Not much. I'm light."

Of course there wouldn't be any scales in a place like this.
Yukari got up off the rock and stood in front of Matsuri.

"*Hoi?*"

"Stand up," said Yukari. "Nice and straight."

"Okay."

Yukari had to tilt her head upward ever so slightly to look
Matsuri in the eye—she must have been one, maybe two centimeters taller. Close enough. Her eyes continued down to her
chest. Mother nature had been generous to Matsuri. Yukari furrowed her brow. From the chest down, Matsuri narrowed considerably—enough to offset the extra weight she carried above.
Her hips were well-rounded, and her legs were long and thin.
There wasn't any fat on her body.

Her proportions may have been a little off, but overall, her
height and weight were almost an exact match. There was no
question that she was fit, and she had spent her entire life in
the jungle, so she could probably *teach* survival training. She
even spoke Japanese and English. If Yukari was qualified to be
an astronaut, there was no question Matsuri would be.

So long as she fulfilled her responsibilities to the space program, she could quit without breaking the terms of the deal with
her father. Then they could go back to Japan together. An under-
handed scheme, but if anyone could handle training hell, it was
Matsuri. It would be a happy ending for everyone.

"Dad?" Yukari said.

"Yes?"

"I need to head back to the base. Do you mind if Matsuri shows
me the way?"

"Not at all."

"I thought I might give her a little tour of the place once we're there. Let her see what kind of technology they have."

"That's a great idea. You'd like that, wouldn't you, Matsuri?"

"*Hoi!*"

"So you don't mind if she's gone a little while? It'll be nice to have someone my own age to talk to for a change."

"She can stay as long as she likes."

"Thanks, this should be fun."

"You ready to go?"

"Ready," said Matsuri.

"Don't forget your promise, Dad."

"How could I? You two be careful."

The chief saw them off and returned to his hut. He walked over to a basket of woven bamboo near the wall and lifted the lid. A mobile phone rested at the bottom. He took it out and pressed the speed dial button.

"Hello, Solomon Space Center? This is the chief of the Taliho tribe. Director Nasuda, please." There was a short pause while the operator put him through. "Ah, Isao. How are you? You were right about Yukari—she just left. Had some interesting things to say. No, no, thank you. We'll be expecting the medicine and cigarettes. We still have plenty of penicillin, but we're almost out of mosquito repellent. The Boonikay? They're not the forgive-and-forget type, and you did bulldoze their land to build your runway. We'll send in a raiding party next week. That should keep them quiet for a while. No, no trouble. Oh, and my daughter is escorting Yukari back to the base. They should be there by tomorrow. Right. Goodbye."

[ACT 8]

MATSURI SAID THE base was close, but it was still a good fifteen kilometers as the crow flies. And the girls weren't flying. Winding their way through the jungle, they had only managed to cover five kilometers in the first day and a half, but the going was much easier once they reached the shore. By the morning of the second day, they could see the base on the far side of the cape. Yukari's spirits soared. Soon she would be through training, and she would be going home with her father in tow. A productive summer vacation by any measure.

Yukari walked happily along the beach, wearing a wreath of flowers Matsuri had made for her during breakfast. Even her space suit felt more comfortable.

When they reached the gates of the base, a group had assembled to welcome her. They must have been monitoring her approach through a telescope. She was greeted with cheers and applause.

"I'm back! Did you miss me?"

Director Nasuda walked up to Yukari. "I see there was no need to worry. Only two days, and back already."

"I have my guide to thank for that." Yukari pulled Matsuri to her side. "This is my sister, Matsuri. I met her in the jungle."

"Nice to meet you," said Matsuri.

"It's sort of a long story, but you can see the similarity, can't you? We're the same height, the same weight—"

The director's eyes went wide. "Satsuki, get over here." He waved impatiently at the doctor. "How much would you say this girl weighs?"

Satsuki's eyes sparkled. "I'd say 38.5 kilograms, give or take."

"Good. And her measurements?"

"Height, about 157 centimeters, 85 centimeters through the chest, 53 at the waist, 84 at the hips." She smiled. "The very picture of health."

"I don't believe our luck." Director Nasuda's face flushed with joy. "I don't think we even need to wait for the tests. We've found out backup crew!"

"Backup?" Yukari's eyebrows shot upward. "What do you mean, 'backup'?"

"We can't let the fate of the entire program rest on a single person. There has to be a contingency plan," said Director Nasuda. "Now everything is in place. We can even use the same capsule. Between the two of you, there's no mission we won't be able to handle."

"It couldn't have worked out better," Satsuki said, her smile wide.

"So, you still need me?" Yukari asked.

"Absolutely. You're our senior astronaut. The honor of the maiden flight is entirely yours. I daresay we may need to extend your tour from six months to a full three years."

"I'm not so sure that will work."

"Nonsense. Your mother won't have any objections. Knowing her, she won't let you come home a day sooner." Director Nasuda chuckled.

Yukari's face twitched.

"What do you say, Matsuri? Want to become an astronaut with your sister?"

"Woo! Do I ever!"

Yukari slumped to the white pavement as it shimmered in the tropical heat.

CHAPTER IV

THE FEAR DIET

[ACT 1]

"RISE AND SHINE, Yukari."

Yukari groaned.

"Come on, time to get up."

Yukari forced her eyes open. "Ugh." Matsuri's grinning face filled her view.

"Satsuki won't be happy if we're late." Matsuri grabbed Yukari by the cheek and dragged her out of bed.

"Ow! I'm up! I'm up!" Yukari was barely out of bed, and the day was already off to a horrible start. She glanced at the clock. "Whoa, 6:50 already?"

Yukari jumped out of her bunk and went into the bathroom. She raced quickly through her morning routine: wash face, brush teeth, change into gym wear. The same thought went through her head each and every time. How can Matsuri be in such a good mood so early in the morning?

Her half sister Matsuri had been her official backup for one month. In the space program, a backup did more than sit around waiting to take the primary astronaut's place if something happened. Having undergone identical training, there was no one who could better understand the needs of their colleagues, so the backup crew supported the flight crew from the ground for the duration of their mission.

The girls shared a room in an attempt to foster a sense of camaraderie. Yukari didn't mind being around Matsuri, but despite sharing a good portion of her DNA, the cheerful girl's behavior often left Yukari scratching her head.

Their training began each morning at seven o'clock. They started with stretching exercises in the gym before swimming four hundred meters in a pool filled with seawater. Matsuri didn't seem to have any trouble with the regimen, but Yukari's low blood pressure made it difficult for her.

Breakfast followed at eight, by which point Yukari felt closer to starvation than hunger. It didn't help that their diet was fine-tuned for their training—fruit, coconut milk, and one slice of toast didn't come close to filling Yukari up.

At eight thirty there was a briefing with their guidance counselor, followed by actual training at nine. They spent mornings in the classroom educating their minds and afternoons in endurance training battering their bodies. For the most part, endurance training consisted of riding the centrifuge, multi-axis trainer, or motion-based trainer and getting spun, flipped, and bounced until their bodies went numb.

Training ended at six, followed by a shower and dinner, which usually lasted until around eight. The rest of the evening was spent with Yukari keeping an eye on Matsuri while doing homework and studying. Then it was lights-out at midnight. Yukari and Matsuri were essentially together twenty-four hours a day.

Today there was going to be a fire test of the main booster in the morning. The test would mark an important milestone for the project, so both Yukari and Matsuri were invited to attend.

There were more than ten flight controllers in the control room, along with Chief Engineer Hiroyuki Mukai and Fuel Specialist Motoko Mihara. Most of them had worked through the previous night, and a dull malaise hung over the room.

"Good morning," said Yukari.

"Morning, you two. We're just about to get this show on the road." Mukai pointed out the window. "That booster is going to put you in orbit. Let's see what she can do." Thick stubble covered his face.

Two kilometers away on the coast, the test pad was visible through the thick bulletproof glass of the control room. The pad was a sturdy-looking structure of exposed concrete that loosely resembled the Arc de Triomphe in Paris. The first stage of the rocket was fixed to the top of the arch, which was ringed with four stories of scaffolding. Thick concrete covered the area beneath the arch to protect against the thrust of the rocket.

"All personnel have cleared the test area," said one of the controllers.

"All right, let's restart the countdown," said Mukai. A large digital clock in the middle of the room began to tick off the seconds.

"T-minus twenty seconds. Activating data recorders."

Racks of recorders began printing out feeds of data.

"Continuing countdown."

"LOX pressure nominal."

"Four...three...two...one...ignition."

Columns of milk-white smoke shot out laterally from the platform. In seconds, the cloud had spread hundreds of meters, billowing up like an angry thunderhead.

An explosion rattled the glass of the control room.

"T-plus fifteen...sixteen...seventeen..."

The booster still roared.

An alarm sounded as a red light winked on the control panel.

"The LOX injector's overheating."

"Cut the LOX!" Mukai shouted.

"The valve is stuck."

"Shut everything down!"

"Controls unresponsive. Temperature still rising. Reaching critical."

"Dammit!" Mukai wheeled on Motoko. "What did you add to the fuel mix?"

"Just a little accelerant. It burns so fast...Didn't I mention it?"

"No, you did *not* mention it."

A ball of orange flame enveloped the test pad.

The shock wave slammed into the control room, sending papers flying off desks. Yukari fell over backward with a yelp. Outside, a crimson mushroom cloud rose into the sky. The upper half of the test pad had been completely destroyed. The control room fell silent.

"Wow, did you see that, Yukari?" said Matsuri. "That was awesome!" She bounced up and down with excitement.

"You do realize, don't you?" said Yukari, her voice low and deliberate. "We're going to be riding in one of those."

"Don't worry. I'm sure it will be just fine."

Yukari sighed. Maybe Matsuri didn't quite understand, but Yukari wasn't going to wait around to be strapped on top of a glorified bottle rocket while they stood back and lit the fuse. If they lost an astronaut in flight, the program would be dead—trouble was, so would Yukari.

[ACT 2]

YUKARI WAITED UNTIL she was alone with Satsuki before popping the question.

"Why are you suddenly so interested in our evaluation techniques?" Satsuki asked.

"I was just wondering. I know I'm the primary astronaut right now, but it's possible Matsuri and me could end up changing places, right?"

Satsuki put her hand on her chin. "It's possible."

"It's just…we've been training together, so I couldn't help noticing that she seems better at all this than me. She's got more stamina. Her reflexes are good."

"Physically she's performing slightly better overall, that's true. Her studies are another matter."

"Yeah, but she's lived in a jungle her whole life. She can already do fractions, and her memory is great."

"Maybe so, but she's hardly up to Japanese high school standards. Kinoshita said he won't be satisfied until she's at least mastered calculus."

"But *I* don't even know calculus."

"Are you worried, Yukari?"

"Worried?"

"Worried Matsuri is going to pass you by?"

"What? That's crazy."

Yukari had set out to get Matsuri moved up, not defend her own position.

"Good. Don't be." Satsuki laughed. "Besides, you still weigh a kilogram and a half less. That alone is enough to secure you the first slot."

"Is our weight really that important?"

"The rocket is stretched to the edge of its performance envelope as it is. If it doesn't make one full orbit, we can't really call it a success, and if the capsule comes down early, that raises a host of safety concerns. So long as you both meet the bare physical and educational requirements, it all comes down to weight."

"You don't say..."

Satsuki checked her watch. "Lunchtime. One word of advice, Yukari. Don't try skipping meals to lose weight."

"Yes, ma'am."

Matsuri was already eating when Yukari got to the cafeteria. The special of the day: pork chops and broccoli. As usual, their meal had already been decided for them.

"Isn't mayonnaise the best, Yukari?"

Yukari watched as Matsuri inhaled one stalk of broccoli after another. She was still mulling over what Satsuki had told her.

She could try slacking off in class and training in hopes of being moved to the backup position. But they had a habit of making her repeat something until she got it right, which meant she would probably end up doing the same thing day in, day out. She would rather end up drifting dead through space.

But there was another problem. If Yukari intentionally tried to sabotage her own chances, her father might hear about it. And the last thing she wanted to do was give him an excuse, any excuse, to back out of his deal to go to Japan.

That left only one option: her weight.

If she could gain one and a half kilograms, she would be in a dead heat with Matsuri. Gain three kilograms, and it wouldn't even be a contest. "Diet time..."

"You say something?" Matsuri looked up at Yukari from across the table.

"Nothing. Forget it. So, uh, Matsuri. Are you happy with the food here?"

"It's delicious."

"Not the taste, the amount."

"I'd eat way more if they gave it to us."

"Same here."

Obviously Yukari wasn't the only one going hungry. She could always reach over and say, "Mind if I eat that?" but she was supposed to be the civilized one. And if she wasn't prepared to leech food off Matsuri, that meant finding another source.

Their caloric intake was strictly limited to 2,750 calories per day, and of that only a paltry eighty-five grams was protein. Satsuki monitored their diets like a hawk, and everyone on the base knew they weren't allowed to go over by so much as a calorie.

Snacks were out of the question. There was nowhere to buy candy and no one she could ask to smuggle some in for her. On their days off they were allowed off the base, but everywhere they went they were accompanied by a security escort. Their weight would determine the success of the entire space program—the lives of everyone on the base depended on it.

But Yukari's life was riding on this too. She would have to take a chance.

[ACT 3]

IT WAS LATE afternoon on the first Saturday in September. Their training for the day was over. Yukari sat in Satsuki's office writing a report, while Matsuri was getting special tutoring in the classroom.

Mukai walked into Satsuki's office. "Hey, we were thinking about going down to Tianjin Restaurant for some dim sum. Interested?"

"Can you give me five minutes?"

"Sure."

"Then count me in," said Satsuki. "What's with that look, Yukari?"

"I wanna go too."

"You know the rules about outside food."

"I'm a growing girl. A little extra every now and then can't hurt."

"The rules are the rules."

"It's not fair." Yukari forced tears from her eyes. "I'm working so hard. The training is killing me, and all that math and physics and electronics is just gibberish. I want my dad to come back to Japan with me so bad—I can't give up." She sniffed and wiped tears from her eyes. "But I'm always so hungry. Sometimes I think I'm going to pass out. Everyone else gets to eat as much as they want, but not me." Yukari buried her face in her arms.

Satsuki stared at her long and hard. "All right," she said. "We'll go hungry together. Go on without us, Mukai."

"But..." Yukari stammered.

Mukai scratched his face. "That's no fun for any of us, Satsuki. Give the kid a break. A little treat now and then won't hurt anything. Besides, she was too skinny to begin with."

"As chief medical officer, I'm responsible for her weight. Are you prepared to share that responsibility?"

"If she puts on a kilogram or two, I can make up for it in the capsule."

Satsuki snorted. "You're too soft, Mukai." She looked at Yukari. "Fine. Today, and today only, you're allowed to eat off the base. But you'll do it under my supervision, is that clear?"

"Yes, ma'am!" All trace of sadness and tears had evaporated from her face.

Satsuki tidied up her desk and changed out of her white doctor's coat and into a cardigan. "Shall we ask Matsuri to join us?"

"Erm..."

"What is it?"

"Her tutoring isn't finished yet."

"I'm sure if I ask Kinoshita to cut things short today, he won't mind giving her a little extra homework to make up for it."

"But homework is no replacement for one-on-one tutoring."

"Try and put yourself in her place," said Satsuki. "Just a minute ago you were the one blubbering about starving in isolation."

And so they set out to Santiago in a Humvee. Kurosu sat behind the wheel, Yukari and Matsuri rode in the back, and Mukai, Kinoshita, Satsuki, and Motoko rounded out the party. The jungle rushed past as they made their way to Chinatown.

[ACT 4]

TIANJIN RESTAURANT WAS crowded and bustling. The soft glow of incandescent bulbs illuminated the dining room. The air was filled with a lively mix of Chinese, pidgin English, and Japanese. Dim sum carts squeaked noisily as they made their unending circuits around the room, the dishes inside sending up a steady cacophony of porcelain chatter. In the kitchen it sounded as though the wait staff and cooks were embroiled in a heated argument. A mélange of savory smells rose off plates of steamed food and lingered in the air. It was warm and inviting.

Yukari's group caught Mr. Cheung's eye as soon as they stepped inside. He hurried over to greet them. "Welcome, welcome. *Aiyaa*, today you bring lovely girls to visit. You toughen them up since last time I see them. Right this way." He led them to their table. "You start with some Bolay tea?"

"I thought Genpi tea might be more appropriate tonight," said Satsuki. Genpi tea was a well-known diuretic that was also believed to draw fat from the body.

"Genpi tea. One moment, please." Mr. Cheung soon returned with a small teapot, teacups, chopsticks, and plates.

A woman wearing a *qipao*, a traditional Chinese dress, approached their table pushing a cart. "*Haam sui gaau*, shrimp dumpling." Her accent was so thick it was hard to be sure what she was offering.

"Two baskets of shrimp dumplings, please, Hanrei," said Satsuki.

Hanrei placed two bamboo baskets on the table. "You bring new face tonight."

"That's right, you haven't met. These are our astronauts, Yukari and Matsuri Morita. Hanrei is Mr. Cheung's granddaughter."

"Oh, you astronaut?" Hanrei regarded them with amazement. "Everybody talk about you. You child prodigy!"

"I wouldn't go that far," said Yukari.

"I hear about engine test. Too bad."

"I was really looking forward to that Peking duck," said Satsuki.

Mukai leaned over to Yukari and Matsuri. "Mr. Cheung promised to treat us all to a nice dinner if the test was successful." His eyes moved to Motoko. "Unfortunately, someone had to go and mess things up."

Motoko fired back. "It's not my fault your injector couldn't handle a little extra pressure."

"You leave my rocket out of this."

"If you had used better materials in the first place, we would be eating Peking duck right now."

Their conversation was quickly turning into an outright argument, but the only thing that interested Yukari and Matsuri was the steaming food on the table. Juicy pink shrimp were visible through the slick translucent skin of the dumplings. Their mouths watered.

Yukari stuffed an entire dumpling into her mouth. A salty mix of shrimp and juices burst across her tongue as she bit into it.

Yukari and Matsuri looked at each other.

"This is sooo good," said Yukari.

"More!" cried Matsuri.

Tears of ecstasy filled their eyes. They reached with their chopsticks for another dumpling, but Satsuki stopped them. "You can have one of each dish. That way you get to try a little of everything."

The girls nodded obediently.

Each time Satsuki stopped a cart, she ordered the lowest-calorie items she could find: steamed meatballs, shark-fin dumplings, tapioca pudding, almond jelly.

The parade of food captivated Yukari, but then she remembered why she was there. At the rate things were going, she would never close the weight gap between her and Matsuri. Eating out every once in a while wasn't going to help her pack on the kilograms. If she was serious about gaining weight, she needed to eat like this every day.

Of course, Satsuki would never allow that.

Yukari pushed away from the table and stood. "Excuse me," she said. Yukari scanned the restaurant for Hanrei's cart.

"Hi, Hanrei."

"Barbecue pork buns?"

"No, actually. Nature calls."

"Ah, this way."

Hanrei led Yukari to the back of the restaurant.

"Could you come in for a second?"

"What?"

"There's something I need to talk about." Yukari grabbed Hanrei's hand and pulled her into the restroom. Once they were alone, she explained her food problem.

"*Aiyaa.* You poor thing."

"Right? So do you think you might be willing to make some deliveries for me?"

"Deliveries?"

"You know, pack up some food and bring it out to the base.

Late at night, so no one sees you."

"That sounds like trouble."

"I'll pay you thirty dollars per delivery."

A change came over Hanrei's face. "Tell me what to do."

"I need you to sneak onto the base at one o'clock in the morning. The hard part will be getting past the fence and the guard tower."

"What if I come from ocean?"

"Perfect! There's a small outcropping of rocks to the west of the docks at the base. You know the one?"

"Yes, I think so."

"I doubt they can see us from the guard tower there. I'll bring a little light so you can find me."

"Okay. What food should I bring?"

"The sweetest, fattiest, highest-calorie stuff on the menu."

"I know just the thing. I bring it to you."

A few minutes later Yukari returned to her seat, the very picture of innocence.

[ACT 5]

THE NEXT NIGHT, Yukari listened to the soft sounds of sleep drifting down from the top bunk. The room was dark, but the glowing hands of her alarm clock showed that it was half past midnight. The coast should be clear.

Yukari slipped out of bed and changed into a T-shirt and shorts. She put her wallet and a penlight in her pocket and moved to the window. She opened it without making a sound. Their room was on the second floor, so she slid down a pipe to the ground. The crunch of sand beneath her feet loud in her ears, Yukari made her way to the beach by the pale light of the moon.

A short distance from the barracks, the guard tower came into view. The tower was mounted with a searchlight whose beam swept the base grounds like something out of an old war movie. Yukari advanced cautiously, moving behind buildings and trees that would provide cover from the watchful eyes of the guards.

After walking for a kilometer or so, she reached the base docks. To the west she could see the black silhouette of the shoreline. The coast was rugged and uneven there, though Yukari was unsure whether it was coral or rock. The outcropping jutted several meters above the waterline. Finding a spot that would keep her hidden from the base, she sat down and waited.

It wasn't long before a tiny boat appeared on the water, outlined against the bright reflection of the moonlight that played on the waves. Yukari flashed the penlight. The boat made a beeline for her position. It was a long, narrow canoe with one person seated in the middle, propelling the boat with a slender pole. The canoe was fitted with an outboard motor, but it was lifted out of the water—the sound would only attract unwanted attention.

"Hope you not wait long." It was Hanrei. The canoe pulled up against the outcropping, where she moored it to a nearby rock. Yukari helped her ashore.

"Thanks. That couldn't have been an easy trip."

"No problem." Hanrei took a round bundle from inside the canoe.

Yukari shone her penlight on it, revealing two bamboo baskets filled with assorted Chinese pastries.

"Awesome."

"Big one is pork bun, yellow one is custard tart, and steamed bun filled with white bean paste."

"They look delicious." Yukari reached for the baskets, but Hanrei snatched them away.

"Thirty-nine dollar, please."

"I thought we said thirty?"

"That's the delivery fee. Food extra."

"All right, fine." Yukari produced a handful of bills from her wallet and handed them to Hanrei. By local standards it was a princely sum, but for Yukari, who earned two thousand dollars a month, it was manageable.

Twenty minutes later, Yukari had devoured the food. Full at last.

"Ah, that ought to put some meat on me."

"Good, good."

"I'll see you again tomorrow then?"

"I'll be here." Hanrei untied the canoe with a practiced hand and leapt aboard. She pushed off the rocks with her pole, and the canoe slipped silently into the waves.

It was after two o'clock when Yukari returned to the barracks. Matsuri was still sleeping like a baby. Yukari fell asleep as soon as her head hit the pillow. The next thing she knew, it was morning.

"Rise and shine, Yukari."

Matsuri's smiling face stared down at her. Yukari pulled the covers up over her head.

[ACT 6]

THE NEEDLE ON the altimeter climbed steadily. The attitude indicator was level with the horizon. Yukari's capsule was in the final stage of entering orbit—simulated orbit. The simulator mimicked the actual capsule down to the last button. The control room could manipulate each and every readout and indicator to display whatever the day's training required.

"Altitude, 180 kilometers. Cabin pressure, um, four hundred.

Power at twenty-four volts." Yukari rubbed sleep from her eyes as she read off the indicators. Most of an astronaut's job consisted of reporting data like this.

"Acceleration 7.5 G. Vibration decreasing. Prepare for main booster shutdown." Kinoshita's voice was cool and measured through the speakers in Yukari's helmet. The simulator didn't replicate acceleration and vibration, thus the verbal cues.

A red light appeared on the control panel.

"Uh, capsule separation is red. All other indicators are green. Roll zero. Pitch for orbital insertion. Cabin temperature seventeen—"

"You idiot!" Kinoshita's voice crackled over the speakers. "The capsule failed to separate. Care to implement emergency procedures to fix that?"

"Oh, right. Let's see..."

"Second fuse panel, emergency capsule separation on!"

"Got it. Done."

"And?"

"And what?"

"What is the status of the capsule separation indicator?"

"Green."

"Do I have to ask for readouts now?"

"Sorry."

"That's enough, you're through for today. Let's put Matsuri in."

"Okay."

Yukari disconnected the cables from her skinsuit and removed the seat harness. The simulator hatch opened. Matsuri stood outside, smiling as always.

She laughed. "He really let you have it, huh?"

"Hope you have better luck than I did."

It was one week since Yukari had begun her midnight snacks. She and Matsuri sat as Satsuki gave them their posttraining debriefing.

Satsuki leafed through some papers. "Your performance is

suffering lately—you especially, Yukari. Your concentration and endurance are down two points."

"That's weird," said Yukari.

"Any idea what might be causing it?"

"I can't think of anything."

"Are you getting enough sleep?"

"Same as always."

"Strange."

"I do feel like the fatigue is starting to catch up with me."

Satsuki tilted her head. "You've also been gaining weight."

"Huh?"

"In the last week, 0.6 kilograms—still within acceptable limits."

"Better watch what I eat."

Yukari's plan was working. She gave an inward shout of joy.

"You too, Matsuri."

"*Hoi?*"

"You're up 0.7 kilograms."

Yukari looked at Matsuri in disbelief. What was she up to?

"That's a surprise." Matsuri was cool as a cucumber.

"Your nutrient intake and exercise regimen haven't changed, so why are the two of you putting on weight?"

Yes, why *was* Matsuri putting on weight?

"You haven't been sneaking sweets, have you?" asked Satsuki.

"Not me," said Matsuri. If she was hiding something, she hid it well.

"What about you, Yukari?"

"Of course not."

Satsuki looked at them doubtfully. "I'll give it another week. But if this trend continues, I'll have to reassess your diets. Cut back on your food."

"No way!" Yukari said.

"We'll cross that bridge when we get to it. That's all for today."

[ACT 7]

PRIMARY AND BACKUP were practically inseparable. The girls were together twenty-four hours a day, which meant the only time one could get a jump on the other was while they were supposed to be asleep—exactly as Yukari had done. One thing was certain. If Matsuri kept gaining weight, Yukari would never close the gap, and Satsuki would order their caloric intake reduced.

That night, Yukari canceled her usual delivery and lay in bed, fighting off sleep. She had gotten by on four hours a night while studying for her high school entrance exams, so she could do this now.

A noise roused Yukari from a light sleep. Yukari checked the clock. Three in the morning. There was no sound coming from Matsuri's bunk. Yukari peered into the darkness. Matsuri was gone. Even her old grass skirt and spear were missing.

Yukari changed as quickly as she could and climbed out through the window. The waning moon still afforded some light. As Yukari's eyes adjusted, she could see someone near the ocean, about one hundred meters away. A spear rested on the person's shoulder—it had to be Matsuri. Yukari followed, as silently as she could.

Matsuri made a beeline for the beach, making no effort to conceal herself. She walked past the docks and onto the rocky shore. There would be plenty of places for Yukari to hide, so she closed the distance between them. Matsuri stood atop a large stone, waves breaking against its base. She faced the ocean, spreading her arms as though to embrace it.

Matsuri began to chant in an unfamiliar tongue—half song, half summons. Her soft voice seemed to tease and tickle the air as it rolled out over the calm waters, a sad and plaintive melody.

Something leaped out of the water. *Splash.* Scales glimmered in the moonlight. A school of fish had begun to gather in the shoals beneath the rocks. Matsuri ended her song and leveled her spear.

"Hup!" The spear flashed. "Hup! Hup!" Three fish wriggled on the end of her spear.

Yukari watched in befuddled awe.

Matsuri stood her spear against a rock and went about gathering driftwood, which she then lit with a lighter from her survival kit. She sat cross-legged and skewered the fish on slender sticks of driftwood before arranging them around the fire. The smell of roasting fish filled the air. Mystery solved.

"I don't believe it."

"Oh, Yukari. Want some fish?"

"Don't 'want some fish' me! It's the middle of the night. What do you think you're doing?"

"I woke up, and I was hungry. Is that why you're here too?"

"No!" Yukari stormed toward the fire. "I was watching you to see how you were gaining weight."

"Oh." Matsuri shrugged and bit into one of the fish.

"Stop that!" Yukari grabbed the fish out of Matsuri's hand.

"What was that for?"

"You know we're not allowed to have snacks."

"Taliho eat when we want to. It's not a snack, it's a meal."

"Don't play cute with me."

Matsuri grinned. "You've been gaining weight too, haven't you?"

"So what if I have?"

"When you wake up, you smell like Tianjin Restaurant." Matsuri bit into the second fish.

Yukari watched for a few seconds before grabbing that fish from her too. "I said, stop that."

Matsuri looked annoyed. "Why?"

"If we keep gaining weight, they'll give us less to eat."

"Eat when you want to eat. Dad says that's the key to happiness."

Matsuri reached for the purloined fish. Yukari yanked them out of reach. Matsuri tackled her, and they both went tumbling to the ground.

"So, what's all the fuss?"

Yukari and Matsuri froze. They looked up to see a man towering over them.

"Mr. Kinoshita." Despair clutched at Yukari.

"Care to explain what you're doing out here?"

"It was such a nice night." To her own surprise, Yukari's voice remained level and calm. "We were admiring the moon."

Yukari and Matsuri scrambled to their feet. Kinoshita didn't move a muscle. He stood silent as a statue, gazing up into the sky. His eyes were fixed on the moon.

"I was in high school during the Apollo program," he said. "About your age. All we had was a black-and-white TV with bad reception, but I was glued to it. Armstrong, Aldrin, Collins—they were my heroes. I didn't delude myself into thinking I'd ever walk on the moon myself, but what they did never left me."

The girls listened in silence.

"We may barely be able to reach low earth orbit now, but once we get the LS-7 working, we'll be able to rendezvous with satellites in geosynchronous orbit. From there, putting something in lunar orbit isn't that big of a jump. When Nasuda told me his plans for the program, my heart skipped a beat."

"Would you go? To the moon, I mean."

"I'm in my forties—a bit late to start." A sad smile spread across his face. "But I never ruled it out. Right after the base was up and running, I had them test me—played it up as a joke." Kinoshita fell silent. A wave crashed against the shore, then another. "I'll never forget the look on Satsuki's face when she told me I had an arrhythmia. I think she took it harder than I did."

The smallest problem with his heart, something that had no

effect on his day-to-day life, had crushed this man's dreams.

Kinoshita's voice returned to normal as quickly as it had changed. "There's nothing more important to an astronaut than his health. That means getting enough sleep, and no snacking. That goes for you too, Matsuri. I don't care what the Taliho call it, this is a snack. Don't let it happen again." He raised his voice. "Now get to bed."

Yukari turned Kinoshita's words over in her head as they walked back to the barracks. She had figured ordinary people might be jealous that she was an astronaut— they didn't know any better. But until that night, she had never expected to find those feelings from someone in the program, someone who knew everything she was going through and longed for that dream in spite of it all.

CHAPTER V

PERFECT BY REDESIGN

[ACT 1]

THANKS TO A last-minute equipment failure, Yukari and Matsuri had the day off.

"Let's go for a swim," said Matsuri. "I love the way the water feels."

"I'm there."

In their free time they often went swimming in the ocean, partly because there wasn't anything else to do, and partly because the clear blue waters of the atoll really did feel good.

Yukari and Matsuri bundled towels and swimsuits into a knapsack and set off from the training center. They walked side by side along a paved road that led to the beach. It was the middle of the day, but the sprawling base was silent.

Yukari stopped.

"What is it?" asked Matsuri. Yukari's attention was fixed on a building on the right side of the road. "Is something wrong?"

"Go on without me."

"Why?"

"I'm going to check out the VAB."

"Okay."

Matsuri gave Yukari a puzzled look and continued on to the beach.

The Vehicle Assembly Building—more commonly referred to as the VAB—was the largest building on the base. It looked like two giant matchboxes pushed up against each other, one standing upright and the other on its side. A thirty-meter-tall mobile launchpad was parked near the taller part of the structure. That was where the various stages of the rocket would be assembled into a single unit.

Yukari approached the low end, where the individual components were made, and walked up to a guard at the entrance.

"Do you know where they're building the capsule?"

"You mean the manned orbiter?"

"Uh-huh."

"Hang a left up there, and it's the clean room straight ahead. What's the purpose of your visit?"

"Just taking a look."

The guard frowned. "Only authorized personnel are allowed inside. You'll need clearance."

"Authorized personnel? Do you know who I am?" She made no attempt to hide her annoyance.

"Of course, but—"

"Then there shouldn't be any problem."

Yukari started walking toward the clean room.

The guard called after her. "Whatever you do, don't go inside. If any outside air contaminates the room, they'll make a fuss like you wouldn't believe."

"Yeah, don't worry. I know what I'm doing."

Yukari didn't have the slightest idea what she was doing. She walked down the corridor for two hundred meters before finally arriving outside the clean room. It was a spacious room enclosed

in glass. Inside, technicians dressed all in white busied themselves
on equipment at the room's center. The entrance to the room was
an air lock with a door at either end. A sign on the outer door read
No Unauthorized Access.

Yukari tapped on the glass. One of the technicians approached
and lifted an intercom receiver. Yukari lifted the corresponding
receiver on the outside of the glass.

"Can I help you?"

"I wanted to take a look at the capsule."

"Observation requests have to go through Mr. Mukai. He's in
a meeting right now."

"So I can't come in?"

"Once you go through the proper channels, there shouldn't be
a problem."

"I'm the one who's going to ride in that thing. Shouldn't I be
able to see it if I want to?"

"It's not that. I'm sure Mr. Mukai will let you watch as much as
you like. Right now, the shield isn't in place, and—"

"Are you trying to hide something from me?"

"Hide something? Of course not."

"You're trying to hide the capsule that my *life* is going to de-
pend on from me?"

"Look, we're not trying to hide anything. The shield just isn't
ready right now."

"Stop making excuses and let me see it."

Yukari dashed for the air lock. She pressed the button frantical-
ly, but the door wouldn't budge. In desperation she tried to force it
open. If someone had asked her why she was doing it, she couldn't
have answered. She had only intended to spend some time away
from work at the beach.

By the time she had forced the first door open, three technicians were waiting for her on the other side. She struggled against
their efforts to restrain her, but in vain.

[ACT 2]

"WITH RESPECT TO yesterday's incident in the VAB," said Satsuki, addressing a meeting of the department heads, "it is regrettable Yukari was not more familiar with clean room procedures. I dropped the ball on that."

"And as a result she came strolling in wearing street clothes," said Mukai, shaking his head. "Not that you can blame her. She doesn't have the slightest idea the danger a speck of dust or a stray hair can pose in space."

"Exactly. As ship's captain she wants the authority to ensure that it's safe." Satsuki turned to Director Nasuda. "She would also like permission to attend the engineering meetings to monitor our progress and voice her opinion."

"Showing some initiative, eh?" said Director Nasuda, clearly pleased.

"I don't have the slightest idea what triggered it, but she's finally starting to take the mission seriously."

"I knew the girl had potential."

"But it will all go over her head," said Mukai. "We're busy enough as it is. If we have to start explaining basic things like elastic deformation to her, we'll never finish."

"Put yourself in her shoes," said Nasuda. "Would you want to climb into some strange contraption on the word of a handful of scientists?"

"Even so."

"Astronauts have always been a demanding lot—comes with the territory. Just because this particular astronaut is a teenage girl doesn't mean we can get away with treating her like one. We have to do whatever it takes to get her on board, if you'll pardon the pun." Director Nasuda looked at the department heads seated around the conference table. "I think we should grant her request. What about Matsuri?"

"She doesn't seem to be the least bit interested," said Satsuki.

"There you have it. I'll tell Yukari our decision myself."

"Yes, sir."

[ACT 3]

THE NEXT DAY Yukari paid another visit to the VAB. Under technician supervision she scrubbed her face, changed into a white suit, and took a 150-kilometer-per-hour air shower to remove stray dust. Mukai greeted her inside the clean room.

"You didn't waste any time, did you?"

"I guess not," Yukari said, a little embarrassed.

"The simulator you've been training in was built for Yasukawa, but this is 100 percent custom-made for you."

Mukai motioned her toward the middle of the room. He may have complained about how much trouble explaining everything to Yukari would be, but there wasn't an engineer alive who wasn't thrilled when someone went out of her way to see the fruits of engineering design.

A conical object the shape of a teepee sat atop a workbench at the heart of a tangle of cables. The interior was still bare, but already it was clear that this was the capsule—the manned orbiter that would carry Yukari into space. It was two meters in diameter at the widest point and three and a half meters tall. The living space inside was the size of a large doghouse. Black heat-resistant tiles covered the pancake-shaped base of the capsule.

"Should there be that much space between the tiles?"

"We did reentry tests on the design last year. The tiles expand when they're heated, so it turns out we actually *need* to leave a little gap between them."

Yukari had demanded to be let into the clean room, but now that she was here, all she could do was listen and nod. She decided that if she could convince herself everything was safe, it would be worth the trouble.

She peered inside the capsule. "So that's what's underneath the control panel. Is the sequencer in there too?"

"Sure is. The computer, communications equipment—all those modules are stored together there, in the avionics bay."

"If something in there breaks down while I'm in orbit, I'm screwed, huh?"

"Not quite. In the unlikely event of a failure, we can cut off an individual module to allow for manual override. So you basically take over for the computer."

"Then I'm definitely screwed."

"Don't worry." Mukai smiled reassuringly. "That equipment isn't going to fail on you. It's flown in the past."

"So what parts *haven't* flown yet?"

"Well, you see—"

He cut himself short, but Yukari wasn't going to let him off the hook that easily.

"Go on, tell me."

"It would take some time to get into that."

"Just how many are we talking about?"

Mukai squirmed under her withering glare. "It's not the quantity that's the problem."

"What then? Let's hear it."

Yukari had slowly backed Mukai up against the wall.

"If I tell you, can you keep it secret?"

"Yeah."

"It's the solid rocket fuel for the main booster."

"The big candle-looking thing?"

"You saw what happened in the last test. They're progressing too fast."

The last test had ended in a spectacular explosion because the propellant had burned *too* well, compromising the structural integrity of the rocket.

"I thought progress was good."

"More isn't always better. Rocket science is a conservative field built up carefully over time. Progress is one thing, but when you start making changes and flying cutting-edge technology, there are risks."

"So why not just use the old fuel?"

"Oh, I've asked them to. One day they don't have the formula, the next day the facility they used to manufacture it has been dismantled—she always has some excuse."

"You mean Motoko."

Mukai nodded.

"Refuse to use it then."

"I would if I could," said Mukai. There was real worry on his face. "Truth is, we need Motoko. She has a real gift. The LS-5 isn't half as tall as the H2—it's not much more than a glorified missile. The only way a rocket so unremarkable is going to get someone into orbit is by using a very remarkable fuel."

That afternoon, Yukari had a lot to think about as she left the VAB.

[ACT 4]

SATSUKI SAT AT her desk, arms resting comfortably on her chair, laughing with abandon. "Ask Motoko to stop improving the fuel?" She made a dismissive wave. "Impossible."

"But why?" protested Yukari.

"There is no why. That's just how Motoko is. You could as soon ask a fish not to swim. That's the reason I recommended her in the first place."

"*You* recommended her?"

"The director needed a top-notch chemist. Motoko was a researcher at a pharmaceutical company at the time. Director Nasuda made her an offer she couldn't refuse."

"How did he do that?"

"He knew her one weakness."

Then and now, Motoko Mihara was only interested in one thing: oxidation, the combination of various chemicals with oxygen. In other words, burning things. With enough oxygen you could burn just about anything, even steel. Motoko was never happier than when she was watching that transformation take place.

"A rocket burns one ton of propellant every second," Director Nasuda had told her. Motoko swallowed hard. "Suppose I want a low mass gas to generate a jet of high-speed thrust. What do I use?"

Motoko answered without hesitation. "Hydrogen."

"That's right. But we're not using hydrogen. Our rocket's going to be a hybrid—solid fuel, liquid oxidizer. So we need a material that's solid at room temperature, inexpensive and readily available, and produces high thrust relative to its mass." Director Nasuda stared hard into her eyes. "Find that material for me, and you can run your lab however you like."

"When do I start?"

Motoko had spent the next month getting her affairs in order. Then, leaving her husband to fend for himself in Japan, she had set out for Maltide.

"And that's why there's no calling Motoko off her research."

Yukari inclined her head. "I don't know how someone like her ever got married."

"There aren't a lot of women in that field. I hear she was very popular."

"Really?"

"Really."

Yukari inclined her head again. Maybe underneath those glasses Motoko was actually pretty.

"She told me one day she just decided to get married, and that was that. But she never played housewife, never had any kids— whatever her reasons were, I couldn't begin to guess. But there's no stopping her. Let it rest."

[ACT 5]

YUKARI WASN'T ABOUT to let it rest. Did Satsuki think she was a soldier they could just order around?

Yukari called security and had them send over a patrol car to pick her up. What was the point of being an astronaut if you couldn't throw your weight around?

"Fuel Processing Center, please."

"Yes, ma'am." The younger security officers never asked questions if you spoke in a firm voice.

When they reached the Fuel Processing Center, Yukari went straight to Motoko's lab. She wrinkled her nose at the strong smell of acid in the room. Flasks, test tubes, and beakers brimming with exotic chemicals covered every desk, table, and even parts of the floor. Anyone unfortunate enough to trip would be in for a visit to the emergency room.

Motoko, however, was not there. Someone in the hall informed Yukari that she was in the indoor jet and rocket test facility. According to the building map, the test facility was a giant chamber with an oversized exhaust duct.

A blast-resistant hydraulic door awaited Yukari at the entrance to the test facility. The door was closed, and an illuminated sign read TEST IN PROGRESS. Ignoring it, Yukari pressed the OPEN button beside the door.

A surge of heat that might have been from the furnaces of hell slammed into Yukari. She leapt behind the door to hide from the terrifying roar and blinding light. The flood of sound and light held steady—at least she hadn't blown up the building. Thirty seconds later, everything went quiet. Cautiously, Yukari peered inside.

Wisps of smoke rose from an engine. Motoko stood nearby wearing ear protectors, her back to the door. She was alone, still as a statue. After a few moments, her shoulders began to shake. She was laughing. A small titter at first, then a roar that echoed through the test chamber. "I did it!"

Yukari stepped into the room. "Excuse me, Motoko?"

"I finally did it."

"Hello in there!"

Motoko continued her celebratory dance, oblivious. Yukari walked up behind her and unceremoniously ripped the ear protectors off her head. Motoko spun around. She wore tinted welding goggles, which she then stripped off, revealing her familiar thick glasses.

"Oh, Yukari. I didn't hear you come in."

Yukari took a deep breath. "I have a question to ask you."

"What is it?"

"We're just two months away from launch. What are you doing in here?"

"Perfecting the fuel we're going to use."

"Not anymore you're not."

"Why?"

"Rocket science is a conservative field..." She recited Mu-kai's speech as best she could. "Stick with what we know," she concluded.

"But this mix is much better than the last one. I adjusted the oxidizer, and—"

"This isn't a request. It's an order."

"After all the trouble I went to?"

"We're using the last formula."

"No no no!" She shifted her weight uneasily from one foot to the other. "Besides, I've already forgotten the last formula. We can't go back." Excuses, just as Mukai had said.

"I don't want to hear it," said Yukari. "I guess we'll just have to see what everyone at the engineering meeting has to say." Yukari had real power now. And she liked it.

[ACT 6]

THE SOUND OF heels on tile echoed through Tianjin Restaurant. "Does anyone here speak Japanese?" A woman stood in the entrance. She wore a dark red suit with a tight skirt, but despite the sweltering heat, not a drop of sweat marred her face.

Mr. Cheung greeted her. "Welcome to Tianjin Restaurant. My name is Tianjin Cheung. This is my restaurant. Japanese love my food."

"Maybe later. Right now I'm trying to reach the Solomon Space Center. Is it possible to get there by train or bus?"

"*Aiyaa.* No train. No bus."

"Then perhaps you could arrange a car for me?"

"I'm not taxi service."

"I'll pay, of course. One hundred dollars."

"One moment, please. Have seat." Mr. Cheung shouted to the back of the restaurant. "Hanrei! Customer need *pullycar.*"

"And hurry, would you? I don't have much time."

[ACT 7]

THE ENGINEERING MEETING started two hours later. Various department heads filled the room. Yukari tried to recall her time as class president in middle school to calm her nerves. She began in a solemn tone. "I've asked you here today because I've uncovered a matter that poses a grave threat to the safety of the mission." The assembled men and women regarded her coolly. "My investigation has uncovered that one of the departments is attempting to independently modify the design specifications of the rocket. Chief Engineer Mukai assures me that rocket science is a conservative field built up carefully over time. Am I quoting you correctly, Mr. Mukai?"

"Uh, yes, that's right."

"Then you can imagine my confusion when I witnessed the test of a new solid rocket fuel this afternoon at the Fuel Processing Center."

Yukari surveyed the crowd.

Director Nasuda made a show of folding his arms. Mukai scratched his head. Satsuki cleared her throat. Kinoshita sat unfazed. And then there was Motoko, looking nervously from one person to the next, measuring the reaction of her peers.

"The chief of the chemistry department, Mrs. Mihara, told me that the fuel she was testing was to be used in the upcoming launch. She assured me it was 'much better' than the old formula. But with only two months remaining, what assurances can we really have? More isn't always better. So where does 'much better' leave the safety of the rocket? In light of this, I hereby request that all research on and use of new fuels be stopped immediately."

Yukari sat down. Let them argue with that.

Director Nasuda broke the silence that had descended on the room. "You heard the lady. Reaction? Let's start with you, Kinoshita."

"Her reasoning is sound. I'd say she's struck on a real problem."

"Hmm. Mukai? What about you?"

"Well, the LS-5 is underpowered, we all know that, and it's a little late to consider adding an auxiliary booster. It *would* be nice to squeeze a little more thrust out of the fuel..."

"Stop mincing words."

"At this stage, going back to the drawing board is too risky. We need to stick to the original design."

"Noted." The director faced Motoko. "What do you have to say, Mihara?"

"Um, right. Well, there's something I want you to see first." She stood up, hastily gathering the materials she had prepared for the meeting and walking to the overhead projector at the back of the room. The lights went dark, and a hand-drawn molecular diagram appeared on the screen. "This is the chemical composition of the new fuel. It has a natural rubber base combined with ample quantities of methylene—"

"Yes, yes," said Nasuda. "How does it perform?"

"I was getting to that." A hint of a smile spread across her face. "For solid fuels, the entire tank containing the fuel is essentially a high-temperature, high-pressure combustion chamber, which adds considerable weight to the launch vehicle."

"Which is precisely why the rest of the world has adopted

liquid fuel launch systems, we know this. We went out of our way to use solid fuel to save on costs, so we could launch lower-cost vehicles in greater numbers."

"That's right. Only this new fuel actually weighs less than the liquid alternative."

The room fell silent.

"That's absurd," said Mukai. "I don't care how light you make the fuel, it's the weight of the tank that's the problem."

"This particular fuel burns from the inside out," said Motoko. "Particulate cohesion is greater toward the outer edge—the fuel is essentially its own container."

Director Nasuda's ears perked up. "What?"

Kinoshita arched his eyebrows. "You developed a tankless fuel?"

"More or less. It still requires some sort of casing—a three-millimeter duralumin sheath is more than adequate."

Mukai was speechless. The mood in the room had shifted dramatically. Yukari was getting worried.

"I find that hard to believe," said Kinoshita. "I don't see how a fuel could be that strong and still burn."

"I had to adjust the catalyst to compensate. It's composed primarily of platinum."

Yukari's eyes went to Motoko's left hand. There was a mark where her wedding ring had been.

"If the walls of the tank are three millimeters thick," Mukai said, tapping on his calculator, "that would reduce the mass by a factor of thirty! A liquid propellant rocket couldn't come close."

"How soon could you prepare fuel for testing?" asked Kinoshita.

"Two months should be plenty of time."

"No time for a dry run."

"We can do a ground test before—"

Yukari sprang to her feet. "Hold it! It's too dangerous to go back to the drawing board with only two—"

Mukai cut in before she could finish. "But this is a breakthrough.

A light, inexpensive, hybrid rocket that can be throttled—it's the ultimate launch system. Tell her, Nasuda."

His face stiff, Director Nasuda slowly nodded. "If this is real, we're looking at a revolution in rocket materials science." He spoke in a hoarse whisper.

"We'll be making history," said Kinoshita.

"Not you too!" cried Yukari, her voice shaking. "What's the matter with you people? You think I'm going to let you test your rocket on me? Forget it! What happened to safety? What happened to building step-by-step on proven technologies?"

None of the department heads could look her in the eye.

Finally, Mukai spoke. "Our current rocket has risks of its own. We're pushing it to the very limits of its capabilities. In a way, this new fuel would reduce that risk. Back me up on this, Kinoshita."

"You do have a point," Kinoshita conceded.

"Here's what we'll do," said Director Nasuda. "There's no need to rush this. Let's see how things develop and make our decision once we have a little more to go on. With full consideration for the opinion of our young astronaut, of course."

"We're going to decide *now*," growled Yukari. "I'm against this 100 percent. Remember who's going to be riding in that death trap of yours. Try and see things from my point of view!"

"Easy, Yukari. We haven't committed to using this new fuel. We simply want time to evaluate—"

Yukari kicked her chair and stormed out of the room.

Not going to use this new fuel? Did they expect her to believe an out-and-out lie like that? Yukari was young, but she hadn't been born yesterday. She might not understand the science behind it, but she saw how they swooned at the idea of this "breakthrough." The angrier she became, the faster the thoughts turned over in her head. As she strode down the hall, she realized what she had to do.

Yukari entered the dressing room and retrieved her skinsuit from one of the lockers. She put on the suit and slipped on an extravehicular activity backpack. So long as the batteries and water supply held out, the EVA pack would allow her to survive for days in virtually any environment.

Grabbing a survival kit, she headed for her desk in the medical office. Matsuri was there studying.

Matsuri looked up from her textbook. "Do we have EVA training today?"

"No." Yukari ripped a calendar off the wall and began writing something on its back with a thick marker. "I'm going to teach them something about being an astronaut."

"*Hoi?*"

"As of now, I'm on a hunger strike. Spread the word."

Matsuri could only stare in wonder as Yukari hurried out of the room.

[ACT 8]

YUKARI SAT CROSS-LEGGED on the concrete, her head resting on her hands. *REDESIGNS KILL! SAY NO!* declared a protest sign taped to the wall behind her. Thirty minutes had passed since she had announced her hunger strike to Matsuri.

"Listen to me, Yukari," said Satsuki. "I understand how you feel, but if you don't abide by the decision made at the meeting, it's tantamount to sabotage." She was using her most persuasive tone. "If you won't listen to reason, I'm going to be forced to report this to your father."

"Be my guest. I'm holding up my end of the bargain. I'll do what's required of me. What I won't do is ride in that jury-rigged experiment you're trying to pass off as a rocket!"

Satsuki shook her head and sighed. At her back, the department heads watched the proceedings from the sunbaked asphalt of the parking lot.

"So much for our trump card," muttered Director Nasuda.

"She has a point, you know," said Kinoshita. "We all went a little starry-eyed at the thought of Motoko's latest invention."

"Even so." Director Nasuda was grim. "If we can put a person into orbit, and do it with a revolutionary lift vehicle to boot, it will turn the global space industry on its head. How can we not use it?"

"I don't disagree, but can't we just let this run its course? What's the longest she can keep this up? Two, three days?"

"If we ignore her, we'll only confirm her doubts about us. No harm in showering her with a little attention."

Satsuki rejoined the group. "I gave it my best shot. Who's next?"

"I'll go," said Mukai. "What we're suggesting may not be by the book, but even from an engineering standpoint, this new fuel isn't all that risky. Maybe I can explain that to her."

"Break a leg."

"So it's like this, Yukari. Since the structure of the fuel provides the necessary strength, it doesn't place any additional burden on the rocket. And of course the fuel itself is safe. You with me so far?"

"Because that's what the specs say, right?"

"Right. So—"

"Well, of course the specs are going to look good on paper. But what happens if something goes wrong when you make it?"

"That's why we have ground tests."

"You expect me to trust a *test*?"

Mukai didn't have an answer for her.

"I don't think I'm on her friends list anymore, Satsuki." Motoko knitted her brow as Mukai came scampering back with his tail between his legs. "I thought she'd be delighted."

"Under different circumstances, I'm sure she would have been," said Satsuki.

"I didn't mean any harm."

"I know. You don't think I'd have let you get away with this if you had."

"But she seems rather upset."

Satsuki tapped Motoko on the forehead. "Your timing leaves something to be desired."

"Maybe I should apologize."

"That would just make things worse. She doesn't want an apology, she wants an answer. She's much more grounded than you, Motoko."

"Grounded?" Motoko considered the word, what Satsuki might have meant by it—but if she reached a conclusion, she didn't share it.

Matsuri joined the crowd in the parking lot. "*Hoi?* What's going on?"

"Yukari's hunger strike—the one you told us about," said Satsuki.

"Right," said Matsuri. "What's a hunger strike?"

"She's refusing to eat until her demands are met."

"But she'll starve. What are her demands?"

Satsuki gave Matsuri a quick rundown of the situation.

Matsuri walked over to where Yukari was sitting. "You don't need to worry."

"So you're on their side too?"

"The launch will be fine. No point going hungry."

"What are you basing that on? Most of the rockets they launch explode, you know that."

"Only because of the Taliho curse."

"The what now?"

"Before each launch, everybody in the village gets together to put a curse on the rocket so it'll explode, like fireworks. Only I'll tell them not to do it when we're aboard. So everything will be just fine."

"Yeah, riiiight."

"I know what you're thinking." Matsuri nodded sagely. "They'll want to see fireworks so much, they'll forget and curse the rocket anyway. But Dad will make sure they won't. It will be fine, I promise. Everybody likes Dad—they'll do what he asks them to."

Yukari sighed and shooed Matsuri away. "Time's up, Tarzan."

"Want me to bring you something to eat?"

"Then it wouldn't be a hunger strike, would it?"

"*Hoi*. See you later then."

As Matsuri hurried away, a security Humvee pulled into the parking lot. The door opened, and there was the dry rasp of heels on concrete. A woman in dark red stepped out and started walking toward Yukari, ignoring the department heads assembled beside her.

Yukari watched, disinterested. Then she did a double take.

"What are you doing here?" asked Yukari.

If there was anyone who would show up at the far corners of the earth without warning, it was her mother.

"I have a Pacifico meeting in Sydney, so I thought I'd drop in on my way. You look good."

"You think so?"

"All slim and toned—and that space suit's adorable. It does wonders for your figure."

"A little too much, if you ask me."

"Don't be absurd."

"Pardon me," said Director Nasuda, "but I don't believe we've been formally introduced."

"I'm Hiroko Morita, Yukari's mother."

"A pleasure. We didn't expect to see you out here so soon. I'm Isao Nasuda, the director of the space center."

"Yes, we spoke on the phone. I was out this way on business, and I thought I'd stop by." Hiroko paused. "I have to admit, I'm a little shocked by what I'm seeing."

Director Nasuda scratched his head. "Yes, well, I assure you, we're doing everything we can to—"

"I expected to see row after row of high-tech buildings. All this exposed concrete is terribly heat inefficient, not to mention unattractive. This is a gateway to space, to the future—it should look the part."

Yukari rolled her eyes. Her mother was an architectural designer; the buildings were always the first thing to grab her attention when she visited someplace new. And if there weren't any buildings, her thoughts went to what might be built there.

Yukari tugged on her mother's sleeve. "If you hadn't noticed, I'm on a hunger strike."

"Oh, the sign? 'Redesigns kill. Say no.' What's that about?"

Yukari explained how the situation had started. They went back and forth, with her mother asking questions about the procedures for launching a rocket.

"I think I understand," said Hiroko. "Are any of the rocket scientists here? One of those people, perhaps?" She pointed to the department heads.

"That's right," said Director Nasuda.

"Do you think I could have a word?"

"Well, I suppose." He waved them over. "A minute of your time, if you would."

"In short," Hiroko began, "my daughter is concerned about using a fuel that has never been flown. It seems to me the best way to address her fears would be to fly the fuel before her launch. Am I wrong?"

"We have to launch Yukari in two months," said Mukai. "That deadline won't budge. It's going to take that long just to prepare the fuel."

"You have two launchpads, don't you? You can build two rockets in parallel—one the test vehicle, the other Yukari's. I'm told it's only six minutes from launch until the rocket reaches orbit.

Launch the test rocket six minutes earlier, and if there aren't any problems, you can go right to Yukari's launch."

"Two rockets? At the same time?"

"I wouldn't stop at two—ten is a nice, round number. It will be cheaper building them in bulk, and since they'll all be made to the same specifications, it will help put my daughter at ease."

"They're not launching *me* ten times," said Yukari.

"Whomever, then." Hiroko turned to Director Nasuda. "If you're really that confident in this technology, it's the only way that makes sense. Throw every yen you have into mass production. Think of how the auto industry handles the release of a new model. They don't make the announcement and then ask their customers to wait while their cars are manufactured. They're ready from day one. Why should rockets be any different? Rockets on demand—the Solomon Space Association's new business model. The world will beat a path to your door."

"Brilliant!" Director Nasuda clapped his hands together. When it came to making the big decisions, no one was faster than Nasuda. "What do you say, Yukari? Will a test launch just before your own be enough to satisfy you?"

"I suppose."

"Motoko, can you produce enough fuel for ten rockets with your current facilities?"

"I should be able to manage," said Motoko.

"Mukai, how many rockets can you crank out?"

"I can probably have the first two ready in time."

"If we reorganize the assembly line right, I bet we can manage three," said Kinoshita.

Mukai put a hand on Kinoshita's shoulder. "Let's slow down here."

"Listen, if anything goes wrong with the test vehicle," replied Kinoshita, "the project is over. The end. Having another backup cuts our risk significantly."

"Three it is then," said Director Nasuda. Subject closed.

"Everyone, I know these next two months aren't going to be easy, but it all comes down to this. Now let's get to work."

When Yukari's mother said she was just dropping by, she had meant it. Her boat back to Guadalcanal left that afternoon. The car Mr. Cheung had arranged for her was waiting at the gate of the base.

"Mom," said Yukari.

"Yes, dear?"

"If you take the base helicopter back, you can see him and still make your boat."

Hiroko shook her head. "Next time."

"Oh. Okay."

She got into the car and rolled down the window. "The hunger strike—that was a good idea."

"You think so?"

"Getting involved with your work is the only way to enjoy it. You have to test your boundaries."

"Yeah, maybe," Yukari said.

"If you're not careful, you might end up liking it."

"Not likely."

Yukari watched as the car disappeared into the jungle.

CHAPTER VI

MIDNIGHT INTERVIEW

[ACT 1]

"ALL RIGHT, LET'S try a shot with the two of you holding your helmets—there, perfect."

Click. Whir. Click. Whir. Click.

The sound of the camera's motor drive echoed through the cavernous Vehicle Assembly Building. The man behind the lens was twenty-six-year-old Tohdo Takeuchi, SSA's new public relations director. He had only held the position for three weeks. While honing his chops on a worldwide photography expedition, he had made a stop at the base and never left. His interest in photography bordered on obsessive.

Takeuchi held his beloved OM-4Ti on its side for a vertical shot.

"Drop to one knee for me, Matsuri."

"*Hoi.*"

"Yukari, stand a little closer, with your left hand on Matsuri's back—that's it."

Click. Whir. Click. Whir. Click.

"Let's see some smiles, Yukari."

"How much longer?" Yukari's expression was sullen.

"We're just about done here. Then I need a few shots of you training—the centrifuge, the simulator, the neutral buoyancy pool." Takeuchi counted off the pending photo shoots on his fingers.

Yukari broke in before he could go any further. "Can't we do those *next* time?"

"I'd like to wrap it up today. Time is tight if we want to make the New Year's Eve specials."

"Who cares about PR? All that matters is if the mission is successful."

"We want the media to give this project the coverage it deserves. That's why I'm putting together a proper press kit—glossy photos, the whole nine yards."

"A press kit?"

"We're sending them out to all the major newspapers and TV stations. They'll include everything from an overview of the program to directions on how to get to the base."

Yukari sighed.

"It's free publicity. That has to be worth posing for a few pictures."

"But it's all so...phony."

"Welcome to PR."

[ACT 2]

"THERE'S SOMETHING WE need to talk about, Yukari." Director Nasuda sat at his desk, chewing slowly on his words. "We're about to step onto the world stage. We may be cloaked in the guise of the OECF, but we both know what this performance is really about—Japan's first independent attempt at manned space-flight. And do you know who the star of our little show is?"

"Me?" Yukari ventured.

"That's right. The youngest astronaut in history, flying solo in a one-man capsule. You're going to be at the center of a global media frenzy."

"I can take it."

"We need you handling interviews with courtesy and grace, no matter what sort of questions they throw at you."

Yukari swallowed hard.

"You're the face of the entire program. The world will see us in the light the media shows us in. It's up to you to ensure that's a positive light. The future of the program depends on it. This is a task every bit as important as your duties as an astronaut. You're sure you're up to it?"

"Yeah, I guess."

"I knew we could count on you. The media will be reporting on every aspect of your life—birthday, blood type, favorite food, relationships past and present."

"I bet."

"But one thing is going to have them worked up more than anything else—your family." Director Nasuda looked Yukari squarely in the eye. "A globe-trotting mother who's an architectural designer. A father who disappeared on his honeymoon and became the chief of a tribe of indigenous Solomon Islanders. A half sister whose mother is a tribal shaman."

Yukari nodded.

"Of course we could...cover this up if we wanted to. Tell them you were visiting the Solomon Islands on vacation. That Matsuri was the granddaughter of a Japanese soldier who had become part of the tribe. It's a small island, so it wouldn't take much effort to lay the groundwork."

"Hmm."

"The cover-up is the easier way. It will let us head off any tabloid reporting that might upset our schedule. It's only twenty days until the launch—you may be handling the pressure now, but there's no need to go asking for more."

Yukari considered for a moment before answering. "I'll take my chances."

"Oh?" Director Nasuda arched his eyebrows. "You want the whole truth out there?"

"I don't like the idea of lying, and what better time to publicize the fact that my family is finally getting back together."

"Interesting."

"We're lucky my mom had the job she did. We always had enough money, and she still managed to bring me up in spite of being a single mother. That has to play well. None of it changes who my father is, but at least I finally found him."

"I doubt they'll leave it at that."

"If the press gives my dad a hard time, it's no more than he deserves."

"They'll make him out to be the bad guy."

"Isn't he?"

Director Nasuda gave an inward sigh. Apparently Hiroshi Morita wasn't done paying for the sins of his wayward fatherhood. "Who am I to convince you otherwise?"

Yukari turned to leave and then stopped. "Oh, one more thing. Do you think you could have them include this family stuff in the press kit? I don't want to go over all the basics every time I sit down for an interview."

"I'll make sure it gets in. The secrecy ends now."

[ACT 3]

BY HELICOPTER IT was less than five minutes from the base to the Taliho village. A large sling lowered Matsuri down to the village square as the helicopter hovered overhead. Once on the ground she rushed up the ladder to her father's hut.

"*Hoi!* It's me, Dad."

"Good to see you, Matsuri." There was real joy in Hiroshi Morita's eyes. "Quite an entrance you made on that helicopter."

"We're so busy with training it's the only way I'd have enough time to visit. I got them to drop me off during our lunch break." Matsuri sat down cross-legged in front of her father.

"Modern conveniences can be nice, eh? So, what brings you here?"

"I don't have long, so I'll keep this short." Matsuri checked her wristwatch—an SSA-issued Omega Speedmaster. "Yukari's launch is scheduled for the twenty-seventh, and they're going to send up a test rocket just before her launch."

"That's wonderful."

"It's really important that nobody places any curses on these two rockets. You can't let anybody turn them into fireworks."

The chief's face was somber. "Of course. We'll have to be careful."

"I'll be in the control room providing mission support, so I can't be here. That means you have to make sure nobody does anything they shouldn't."

"I'll take care of it. We won't curse any rockets between now and December 27."

"Thanks, Dad. Do you know where Mom is?"

"Toto's in the spirit lodge. She won't be out until tonight."

"Oh, okay. I'll come back tomorrow or the next day to talk about this with her."

Matsuri's mother, Toto, was a village shaman. Matsuri wouldn't be able to put her mind at ease until she had explained the situation to Toto as well.

"By all means. So, how is Yukari holding up?"

"She says this is as hard as when she was studying for her high school entrance exams. She can't wait to finish so she can go back to Japan with you."

"That came up, did it?"

Matsuri looked at her father and smiled. "If you don't go to Japan with her, she's gonna be furious. I don't even want to think of the names she'll call you."

"I can only imagine." The chief forced himself to return his daughter's smile. "To be honest, I thought the rocket would have scared her off by now."

"She told me she was focusing on her ultimate goal, not on how hard things were now. Just like before getting into high school."

The chief sighed. "Civilization toughens people up in its own way."

"*Hoi.* Yukari's tougher than she looks."

"But going into space—that's another matter altogether." The chief looked earnestly at Matsuri. "Take care of her. For all the trouble she's causing, she's still my daughter."

"Don't worry, Dad," Matsuri said. "I won't let anything happen to her."

[ACT 4]

YUKARI STORMED INTO Director Nasuda's office and slammed the press kit down on his desk.

A week had passed since the PR photo shoot.

"What's this supposed to be?" demanded Yukari.

"What's what supposed to be?"

"This pack of lies!"

"Which part?"

"Right here."

Yukari pointed to a paragraph in the kit.

The moment Yukari Morita saw the rocket, it was love at first sight. She had dreamed of space since she was a child. Convinced that destiny had brought her to the Solomon Space Center, she went immediately to Director Isao Nasuda and asked to pilot the rocket on its maiden voyage. Struck by her passion, Director Nasuda wasted no time in having his medical staff assess her suitability for the program. The tests confirmed that Yukari Morita possessed singular physical fitness, mental prowess, and stamina. And so the youngest astronaut in history received her commission.

"Since when am I in love with a rocket?"

"A rhetorical flourish."

"It's a lie. Fix it."

"They've already been released."

Yukari couldn't believe what she was hearing.

"Certain aspects of the program are still confidential," said Director Nasuda. "Your skintight space suit, the new rocket fuel—and above all else, the lift capabilities of the LS-5A. If the truth gets out—that it can only carry someone of your diminutive weight—we're ruined. You can't expect us to announce that *we* recruited you because you were the only person we could find who was light enough to launch."

"That still doesn't give you the right to go making up how I supposedly feel about all this."

"It's part of your job. This is a ten-billion-yen-a-year project. We can't go around saying whatever pops into our heads just because it happens to be true."

"Did you ever think it might be smart to run it by the person you were making up this story about first? This isn't the first time you've shown me such a lack of respect, and I'm sick of it. I'm going to tell the reporters whatever I like."

"Wait! Hear me out!" Director Nasuda half rose from his desk as Yukari turned to leave. "This is our dream," he pleaded. Yukari stopped. "This base is filled with people who want nothing more than to go to space, but they can't. Did you ever think about them? The way they see you?"

Yukari thought back to what Kinoshita had said on the beach.

"Everyone here knows you didn't ask to become an astronaut. But do you really hate it so much? No, don't answer that. But know that everyone here wants to believe that deep down inside, you *don't* hate it. This lie is as much for them as it is for the press."

[ACT 5]

ONCE THE SOLOMON Space Center press kits had been sent out, the media response was immediate. After a battle over the rights to the limited satellite bandwidth over the Pacific, the media started pouring onto the island. Broadcast crews carrying oversized luggage, reporters, cameramen—one after another, they came.

There were teams from six television stations in Japan alone, not to mention Kyodo News Service, the big three American networks, CNN—all of the major players. Counting the print journalists who didn't show up with much more than the clothes on their backs, the ranks of the press corps soon swelled past four hundred. After checking in and receiving their credentials, they were given quarters in prefab housing on the base. Portable satellite dishes sprang up like mushrooms after a rainstorm.

The first press conference was held on December 19, one week before launch. The main conference room had been converted for the event, complete with batteries of microphones and cameras. At the center of it all, beneath the blinding floodlights, were Director Nasuda, Yukari, and Matsuri.

Yukari and Matsuri wore pink pantsuits, purchased by the public relations officer himself on a trip to Sydney for that purpose. Even Director Nasuda was dressed to kill in a crisp three-piece suit. The air conditioning worked overtime to battle the equatorial heat, but the room remained uncomfortably warm.

Director Nasuda began the press conference with a short address extolling the virtues of manned spaceflight, the advantages of launch systems that handled humans and cargo separately, and the cost-effectiveness of the new hybrid engine. However, the journalists were clearly much more interested in hearing what the girls had to say.

"I have a question for Yukari," said one of the reporters. He had shown remarkable restraint by waiting a full two seconds after the end of Director Nasuda's opening remarks. "Do you have a boyfriend?"

So this was how it was going to be. It didn't seem like an appropriate question for an astronaut, but the journalist looked dead serious. Ridiculous as it may have been, Yukari was willing to go along with it if it meant getting this over and done with.

"No," said Yukari.

"Who's your favorite musician?"

"ZIMA, stuff like that."

"Favorite food?"

"The shrimp dumplings at Tianjin Restaurant."

"Extracurricular activities?"

"Track and field."

"Blood type?"

"A."

"Any brothers or sisters?"

Yukari froze. "Uh, I think the press kit covered that."

"I'd like to hear it in your own words."

"No, no brothers or sisters."

"What do you do if you get your period in space?" asked a female reporter.

At this point, Yukari decided to tell it like it was. "The urine collector in the suit can handle it, but the launch schedule also takes that into account."

"And if the launch is delayed?"

"In a worst-case scenario, they can always use the backup crew."

"Would you categorize your menstrual pain as severe?"

"I'm not going to dignify that with a response," Yukari snapped. A barrage of strobe lights flashed. Yukari had no doubt those pictures would find their way to magazine covers around the globe.

Next her family life came under the microscope.

"What do you think of your father?"

"I think he's a deadbeat."

The directness of her response elicited a number of surprised gasps.

"So you aren't going to forgive him?" purred a female reporter.

"That's up to him."

"How do you mean?"

"If he makes a fresh start in Japan, I'm willing to consider it."

"What are your plans once you and your father go home? There are rumors you're considering an acting career."

"I intend to go back to being an ordinary teenager."

The journalists laughed.

Yukari didn't see what was so funny.

"Any idea why your father disappeared on his honeymoon?"

"Not really." Yukari had expected the question, but she had never got around to deciding how she would answer it. She certainly didn't believe that nonsense story about shamans and spirits. Had the Taliho kidnapped him? Had he run off after a fight with her mother? She couldn't answer because she had no answer.

"Is it possible your father has some sort of mental disorder?"

It was possible. Why should she deny it?

"Yes."

Another journalist broke in. "So Matsuri is your half sister *and* your backup, is that right?"

"That's right."

"Was there any rivalry between the two of you over who would be the first to fly?"

"None at all."

The journalist eyed Yukari doubtfully. "But if something were to happen to you—an injury or an illness—Matsuri would move into the first slot." There was a time when nothing would have pleased Yukari more, but now she was prepared to do whatever she needed to do to get her father home free and clear. "If that happened, you're telling me there wouldn't be any animosity between the two of you?"

"We're not concerned with who goes first."

"Maybe Matsuri sees things differently."

"I'm not in any hurry," said Matsuri. There was no guile in her words.

"I couldn't help but notice you used the word 'first,' Yukari. So there *will* be additional launches?"

"Sure, why wouldn't there be?"

"Of course there will," said Director Nasuda. "Once our technology matures, we may be looking at launches every week."

The journalists all but ignored Director Nasuda.

"Yukari, you gave the ship its name, *Tampopo*. How did you decide on that?"

"I wanted to name it after a flower, and 'Peach,' 'Sakura,' and 'Sunflower' were already taken."

"You'll be flying alone. Are you scared?"

"The rocket is put together well and I'll be in radio contact with the ground, so I'm not really worried."

"What's the first thing you're going to do when you reach orbit?"

"If there's time, I'd like to just stare at Earth."

"Is that why you wanted to become an astronaut?"

"Well..."

Director Nasuda looked at Yukari imploringly.

"Yes, that's the reason," she said.

"When did you first realize this was what you wanted to do?"

"Elementary school probably."

"What prompted this realization?"

"Uh..." Yukari hadn't thought that far ahead. She racked her brain, trying to remember the details of the first Japanese to ride the space shuttle. "I saw an eclipse."

"That must have been the total eclipse in Okinawa." This reporter knew his astronomy.

Sweat beaded on Yukari's forehead. "I'm not sure. I saw it on TV."

"Ah, of course." That seemed to satisfy him. "Do you plan to continue pursuing your career as an astronaut?"

"Yes. Well, sort of. I still need to finish high school."

"What sort of timescale are we talking about?"

"I need to get back before the next semester starts."

"That can't be easy, leaving all this."

"I want as many people as possible to have the chance I have."

Murmurs of approval rolled through the audience.

Yukari's first foray into public deception was a success. And she was just getting started.

[ACT 6]

"DON'T EVEN THINK about it," said Yukari.

Matsuri stopped with her hand on the curtains. "Why?"

"Because they have telephoto lenses pointed at our window, that's why."

"Oh, right."

The journalists swarming across the base were doing anything and everything they could to catch a glimpse of Yukari's and Matsuri's personal lives. They were prohibited from entering any of the facilities on the base without authorization, including the barracks, but since the journalists themselves were housed on the base, there was nothing to prevent them lurking just outside.

"I'm sure they're making reports right now," said Yukari. "*The lights in their room just came on. They must be back from training.* To them it's all freedom of the press. They couldn't care less about our privacy."

Matsuri picked up her hairbrush and held it like a microphone. "*The people have a right to know.*"

"Yeah," she scoffed. "Who gave them the right?"

"Don't ask me."

"Do you have any homework tonight, Matsuri?"

"Nope."

"What do you say we turn in early?"

"Good idea."

Yukari and Matsuri changed into their pajamas. As they were about to go to bed, their door flew open with a bang and a female reporter with a brilliant halogen halo sprang into the room. A cameraman and lightning technician stood behind her.

"Fujimi Television's guerrilla reporter Keiko Momoi, here. You weren't already asleep, were you? No, of course you weren't." Keiko Momoi's voice dripped with condescension.

"Who said you could be in here?" demanded Yukari.

"Oh, you know."

"Enlighten me."

"We're not here to talk about *me*. Your public wants to know about *you*."

The guerrilla interview had begun.

Yukari appealed to the cameraman. "You wouldn't film us like this, would you?"

Momoi answered before the cameraman had a chance. "I think those pajamas are darling. Did you pick them out yourself?"

Yukari felt drained. The media was only interested in fluff, trivia. Did they really expect her to take these interviews seriously?

On the other hand, if she snapped at her interviewers, she would be playing into their hands, and on camera no less. They could twist Yukari's words to fit whatever portrait of her they wanted to present to the entire world. However vapid this reporter seemed, she was a professional who no doubt had an arsenal of tricks up her sleeve to fool Yukari into saying what she wanted to hear.

Resigning herself to the situation, Yukari decided to answer each question as briefly as possible. "The supply department provided them."

"Oh, you poor thing. They don't even let you pick your own pajamas? You astronauts are on a shorter leash than I thought."

"If you think so."

"You know, there's a rumor going around the base that the capsule can only carry a petite passenger like yourself. Any truth to that?"

"I haven't heard any rumors."

"The rumor isn't what's important. Surely the astronaut piloting the rocket must know the truth *behind* the rumor."

"The rocket's specifications haven't been made public yet, so I can't make any comment."

"We've also heard that because the capsule can only carry the weight of a young girl, you were essentially impressed into service. Can you comment on that?"

"Actually..." Yukari bit her lip. *Time for another lie.* "Actually, I'm here by choice."

"Then it's just coincidence that Matsuri happens to have the same build as you?"

"Matsuri wants to be here too. Isn't that right, Matsuri?"

"Sure is." Matsuri didn't miss a beat.

"And the stories we've heard about a male astronaut who quit the program?"

How much did they know?

"I don't know anything about that," said Yukari.

"It's been suggested that he ran away because the rocket was too dangerous."

"I really don't know."

"I've reviewed the launch records—it's been one failure after another lately. Aren't you worried?"

"The failures were with a different type of rocket."

"And why do you suppose they changed to a smaller, older model at the last minute?"

"I don't know!" bellowed Yukari.

"There's no reason to get upset, dear."

"We're trying to get some sleep, and you come barging into our room trying to dig up dirt and *you* don't think there's any reason to be upset? Get out, all of you! *Now!*"

[ACT 7]

THE CALL FROM Yukari's mother came while she was in the multi-axis trainer. Satsuki stopped the machine and waived Yukari over. Yukari took the call at one of the phones on the control panel.

"Hey, Mom."

"How's my little teen idol doing?"

One sentence and her mother had already set Yukari off. "What do you mean, 'teen idol'?"

"You're a hero back here. The brave teenager who's going to face the rigors of space alone. There's a news van outside the house right now. I'm going to be on *Good Afternoon, Japan*."

"Don't let them talk you into saying anything you shouldn't."

"Director Nasuda briefed me on everything that's out-of-bounds. Our stories should match up just fine."

"That's not what I'm worried about. I don't want to turn on the TV and hear you talking about how I wet my bed when I was five."

"When have I ever said anything that would embarrass you? I'll just be talking about how you're an excellent student who was accepted to a good high school, that you were runner-up at the Shinagawa Track Meet—things like that."

"No! That's exactly what I'm talking about!"

"I don't see what harm it could do. I'm proud of you."

"Just promise me you won't say anything, okay?"

"Well, I've already been on a number of programs—"

"Then don't say anything starting *today*!"

"Don't be so Japanese, Yukari. Show a little pride in your accomplishments. You're an astronaut now—you have to think globally."

"What do I have to be proud of?"

"As stubborn as ever. Fine. That's not why I called. The producer of the show I'm about to be on wants some footage of us talking on the phone. They're ready to record right now."

"Absolutely not!"

"It'll only take a minute. I play the worried mother, you just have to follow my lead."

Bang!

Yukari slammed the phone into its cradle. Seeing that the phone was still in one piece, she picked up a folding chair and brought it down on top of the phone. The base of the phone flipped over, and the cord snapped, sending the receiver skittering to the far side of the room.

Satsuki stood up. "It's okay, Yukari."

"I'm gonna smash this phone to bits."

"Just calm down."

"I *hate* it."

"I said calm down!"

"I! Hate! This! Phone!"

Yukari bashed the phone with the chair again and again.

Satsuki grabbed Yukari from behind and locked her in a half nelson. She reached into her lab coat, pulled out a case containing a syringe, and jabbed Yukari in the right arm in the blink of an eye.

The ketamine went to work at once, and Yukari grew quiet. Satsuki laid her down on a couch and wiped the sweat from her brow.

"You're only human," said Satsuki. She returned her syringe to its case. "Better keep this handy until the launch."

Five more days—and it wasn't just the astronauts who were feeling the pressure. The entire base was stressed to the breaking point.

[ACT 8]

IT WAS TWO o'clock in the morning. The upper bunk shook, and Matsuri's head peered down over the edge, upside down. Her long hair streamed beneath her.

"*Hoi.* Yukari. Trouble sleeping?"

"How could you tell?"

"How could I *not* tell. You're even keeping me awake."

"Sorry."

The nap earlier in the day had thrown off Yukari's schedule. Her body was exhausted, but her mind remained clear and alert.

"Something on your mind?" Matsuri asked.

"Nothing in particular." Yukari sighed.

"You people from the modern world worry too much."

"Yeah, maybe."

"You and me eat together, sleep together, train together—but you're the only one who ever worries."

"Uh-huh."

"Maybe a little magic will help."

"I've had enough magic."

"There's nothing to be afraid of. It's real easy, and it will work, you'll see."

"If there's gonna be a whole lot of singing, dancing, and that sort of thing, forget it."

"Don't worry, it's real simple. And you don't even have to pay me for it."

"I hope not."

"Okay, come on. Get up," said Matsuri, excited.

Figuring she didn't have anything to lose, Yukari played along.

Matsuri opened the window just a crack. "We need a way for the spirits to get inside." She changed out of her pajamas and into her grass skirt as moonlight spilled into the room. "Kneel down over here, Yukari."

Yukari complied without a word. Matsuri stood in front of her, her right hand holding her spear and her left resting on Yukari's head.

Matsuri began to chant in the same singsong melody Yukari had heard that night on the shore. Matsuri gently waved her spear as she sang. The seashell bracelets she wore on her arms rustled softly with the motion.

"Relax," said Matsuri. "It's okay to fall asleep if you get tired."

Yukari closed her eyes. The song seemed to resonate within her. Maybe there was something to this magic after all.

"I'm getting sleepy," said Yukari.

"Then sleep. Good night, Yukari."

"Good night."

As Yukari drifted off to sleep, a reporter burst into the room.

"Asleep! Already? Come on, wake up, Yukari."

"Huh? You again?"

Yukari had left strict instructions with security telling them to keep the media out of the barracks.

This time the reporter had come alone. She was a small woman with short hair, and her skin had been bronzed by long hours in the sun. Yukari thought she looked familiar, but she couldn't remember which station she was with.

To Yukari's surprise, the reporter had neither camera nor recording equipment. The only thing in her hands was a microphone, and even that was nothing more than a prop. Yukari was beyond asking why.

"What made you want to become an astronaut, Yukari?"

Here we go again.

"I came here looking for my dad, and they asked me if I wanted to be an astronaut—they said I was just the right size. So in exchange for taking on an easy part-time job, they promised to help me look for my dad."

"I see. But you've found your father now, yes?"

"Uh-huh. But that good-for-nothing deadbeat said I had to finish the job I started."

"You mean you're *not* here by choice?"

"Not really."

"Then you don't enjoy being an astronaut?"

Yukari shook her head. "The training's a killer, and I don't trust that rocket. It's barely got enough lift to get off the ground. That's why they had to go adding boosters and stuff."

"Why not have someone else go in your place?"

"I thought about that for a while."

"But not anymore?"

"I figure I've come this far and I might as well go into space at least once. And they *have* gone out of their way to make changes for me. Who knows—maybe I've caught island fever too."

"That's great."

"No, it's not. Everybody here is crazy. They never think about how the things they do will affect other people. Not that it's all bad."

"So that part's true—you *do* want to go to space."

"Yeah, I guess..."

"But?"

"But I wish I could say it in my own words. Right now it feels like I'm always trying to sell something. And the lying...It's hard to sound passionate about something that isn't true."

"Well, it's a good thing you didn't have to lie to me tonight."

"Yeah."

"Have a good night's rest, Yukari."

"Thanks. Good night."

"Good night."

The reporter left, and Yukari crawled back into bed. Soon she was sound asleep.

The next morning, Yukari awoke feeling more refreshed than she had in a long time.

"I slept like a log," said Yukari with a yawn.

"*Hoi*. Good morning." Matsuri was already up and dressed.

As Yukari rubbed the sleep from her eyes, memories of the previous night's interview came bubbling to the surface.

"Do you remember that interview from last night?" asked Yukari.

"Nope. I must've fallen asleep. How'd it go?"

"Hmm." Yukari inclined her head. "I don't really remember. Probably the same as all the rest."

Matsuri walked over to Yukari's bed. "You've done so many interviews you can do them in your sleep." She smiled.

"Hooray for me." Yukari sprang out of bed and ran to the mirror in the bathroom. "T-minus four days!" she shouted, pumping her fist in the air.

CHAPTER VII

ENDLESS COUNTDOWN

[ACT 1]

IT WAS EIGHT o'clock in the morning on December 26. Billowing white smoke still hung over the launchpad, but the screen had already switched to a telescopic view of the unmanned rocket.

"T-plus 128, 129. Solid rocket booster burn complete." Kinoshita's words reverberated through the control room.

Already one hundred kilometers away, the rocket flickered and burned on the screen like a tiny torch. Two objects separated from the torch, trailing thin wisps of smoke.

"We have solid rocket booster separation."

Director Nasuda made a slight nod.

From here on out, it was up to the main booster. Everything was riding on Motoko Mihara's new fuel. If the fuel didn't burn exactly as planned, the thin duralumin casing enclosing the combustion chamber would be ripped to shreds.

"Come on," Director Nasuda muttered under his breath. The knuckles of his clenched fists were bright white.

Yukari stared intently at the image on the screen.

The LS-5A mounted with Yukari's capsule, *Tampopo*, stood on the adjacent launchpad undergoing final preparations for launch. If all went well with Pathfinder, the test rocket, it would be Yukari's turn tomorrow.

Since liftoff, 310 seconds had elapsed.

"Main booster burn complete. We have second-stage separation. Kick motor ignition successful. All systems nominal."

The crowd breathed a collective sigh of relief that gave way to a smattering of applause.

"Don't count our chickens yet," grumbled Director Nasuda. "Save the applause until we hear from Christmas Island."

A rocket's success depended on a series of steps. A successful main booster burn was a milestone, but the mission couldn't be classified a success until the unmanned capsule reached orbit.

Eleven minutes later, a call came in from the tracking station on Christmas Island, over 4,800 kilometers away. Kinoshita listened to their report, then returned the phone to its cradle. "Christmas Island has acquired Pathfinder," he said, his voice calm. "Orbital inclination eight degrees, altitude 210 kilometers, speed 7.7 kilometers per second." A smile split his face.

Pent-up joy erupted in rapturous shouts and applause. The controllers hefted Motoko and Mukai into the air.

Director Nasuda beamed triumphantly and thrust out a sweaty palm toward Yukari. "Congratulations. You're up next."

Reluctantly Yukari took his hand. "Thanks," she said. Her palm was sweaty too.

[ACT 2]

ALTHOUGH YUKARI WAS done training, her last day was packed with press conferences, health tests, and meetings to review the flight plan. It all went by in a blur.

Yukari's mind felt numb, as though it were floating outside her body and watching everything from afar. She remained calm and collected through it all, more so than even she would have expected. It reminded her of the night before her high school entrance exams. She had prepared as best she could; now all that was left to do was to wait and see what hand fate dealt her.

"I thought I'd be more nervous," said Yukari.

She turned off the lights and drew back the curtains. The shadowy outline of the training facility and the command center framed a silvery path that led toward the ocean. The launchpad loomed in the distance. Spotlights illuminated the maintenance tower from all sides, limning it in white. The lights of an elevator flickered as it rose and fell through the iron skeleton of the tower.

"I may be the only one getting any sleep tonight." Yukari sighed.

In a room beneath the launchpad, Satsuki was giving Mukai an IV drip. He hadn't slept in three days.

"Isn't there a shot that will make me feel like I just woke up from a nice, long nap?" asked Mukai.

"Afraid not."

Mukai stared up at Satsuki from a folding cot. "What's in that thing anyway?"

"Solita-t No. 3 with a vitamin B and C chaser."

"I don't need vitamins, I need something to wake me up."

"I have just the thing, but you're not going to get any from me," said Satsuki in a tone that brooked no argument. "What you need is rest, and that's not something I can give you. Vitamins are the best I can do."

"I just have to make it until morning. It all comes down to today."

"The best thing you can do right now is sleep. The IV will take two hours anyway. Now get some shut-eye!"

[ACT 3]

SATSUKI GAVE YUKARI a wake-up call at three o'clock in the morning. Outside it was still dark.

Yukari and Matsuri went to the cafeteria together for a breakfast of coconut milk, eggs, and toast. Then it was off to the clinic, where Satsuki took their temperatures, blood pressures, heart rates, and urine samples. Satsuki noted the readings in her medical log and ushered the girls to the director's office.

Director Nasuda greeted them with bloodshot eyes—he hadn't been to bed either—and looked over the medical log. Satisfied, he stood and strode over to Yukari and Matsuri.

"Yukari, you are officially the commander of the Solomon Space Association's first manned mission."

"Yes, sir."

"Matsuri, you are our official backup. You will provide ground support from the control room."

"*Hoi.*"

Director Nasuda looked from one girl to the other. "We're counting on you."

Matsuri headed to the control room, and Yukari made her way to the crew waiting room.

Yukari's preparations began with an enema administered by Satsuki, after which she put on her space suit, tied back her hair, and fastened on her helmet. Two technicians accompanied her to a small vacuum chamber the size of a phone booth to test the airtight seals of the suit. Next they checked the sensors that monitored her temperature, blood pressure, and heart rate. The skinsuit checked out.

By the time the checks were complete, it was five o'clock in the morning. Holding her helmet under one arm, Yukari made her way to the entrance of the training facility. Satsuki led the way, and Yukari was flanked on either side by security personnel. Outside, a security Humvee waited to take her to the launchpad. Throngs of reporters lined the short path to the vehicle.

A barrage of strobe flashes greeted Yukari as she stepped out of the building.

"There she is!" cried one of the television reporters enthusiastically. "Yukari has just exited the training facility wearing a white space suit. She's coming this way!"

"Hold that pose," called another reporter. Yukari stopped in front of the car. "What's going through your mind right now?" he asked.

"I just want to go out there and give it my best."

"Did you get any sleep last night?"

"Plenty."

"Anything you'd like to tell your parents?"

Yukari ignored the question and stepped into the Humvee.

As the door closed, the reporter addressed the camera. "Yukari is looking a little nervous this morning."

The Humvee pulled away. Satsuki shook her head. "That gets old fast."

"Uh-huh."

The car sped past the VAB and followed the rails that carried the mobile launchpad to the launch site. The eastern sky was tinged a deep crimson.

A few minutes later, they were at the launchpad. The rocket still basked in the glow of the floodlights, but even so it was a dark shape against the gathering morning light. Liquid oxygen steamed from the middle of the rocket. There were no reporters in sight.

Yukari stepped out of the car and climbed a long concrete ramp. The engineering team was gathered at the top. She could see their red eyes in the reflected glare of the floodlights.

"Your chariot awaits," said Mukai. "She's ready to fly. You don't have to worry about a thing." He was clearly tired, but he forced a broad smile.

Yukari appreciated the gesture. "Thanks," she said, grasping his hand.

Mukai blushed. "Heh, I'll never wash this hand again."

"It's saying things like that that makes it so hard for you engineers to get a date."

"I'll try to remember that."

Chuckles rippled through the small crowd.

Yukari shook hands with each member of the team in turn, and then she and Satsuki stepped onto the launchpad elevator.

Twenty meters above the ground, Satsuki began her final preflight examination of Yukari. "How do you feel?" she asked.

"Never better. And don't forget your promise."

"What promise?"

"To keep the in-flight medical feed private."

"Oh, right. Not to worry."

"Well, see you when I'm back."

"Good luck."

Yukari walked alone down the access arm that led to the capsule. A technician opened the hatch as she approached.

"Morning," said Yukari.

"The weather reports look good," replied the technician.

"Fingers crossed."

"Here we go." The technician stood behind Yukari and lifted her by the armpits. Yukari slid feetfirst into the capsule.

The front of the capsule faced skyward, so Yukari was seated lying on her back. The seat itself had been built to fit her body perfectly from head to toe. A harness attached to her suit via cables at the shoulder, chest, sides, and knees held her firmly in place. Only her head and arms remained free.

After checking the positions of the switches that controlled the potentially dangerous pyrotechnic systems, Yukari switched on the master power.

Ventilation, ON. Cabin lights, ON.

"Ready to seal the hatch?" asked the technician.

"Go ahead."

Ten centimeters above her head, the hatch closed. Yukari reached up and rotated a handle to lock it in place. There was a small porthole in the hatch—the only window on the entire spacecraft. Outside, Yukari could see part of the launchpad, the face of the technician, and sky.

Yukari gave a thumbs-up sign to the technician, who then disappeared from view.

Yukari was finally alone. She breathed a sigh of relief and looked around the inside of the capsule. It was tight—less a spacecraft than an extension of her suit. There was an instrument panel forty centimeters from her face and beside it a small view screen. To her right was a fuse panel with rows of switches, and to her left was an assortment of manual valves. The attitude control stick was positioned at the end of her right armrest, and the emergency abort handle at the end of the left.

There was barely enough room inside the capsule to blow up a large beach ball. A full-grown man would have trouble just making it through the hatch.

Yukari had spent dozens of hours inside this capsule. She could find each and every switch with her eyes closed.

She flipped on the comm switch. "Mission control, *Tampopo*."

"*Hoi*. We hear you loud and clear." Matsuri's voice bubbled through the speakers.

"Roger that, mission control. The ship's chronometer reads five twenty-seven and twenty seconds."

"Roger, your time checks out. Ready to begin your pre-launch check?"

"Affirmative."

"Pyrotechnic safety switch?"

"Locked."

"Attitude control stick?"

"Locked."

"Emergency abort handle?

"Locked."

As Yukari and Matsuri worked their way through the checklist, the technicians were making their final inspection of the booster. If there were no problems, the rocket would lift off at precisely eight o'clock.

At 6:38 AM, Yukari and Matsuri had just finished going through the fifty-page checklist.

"How's the countdown going?" asked Yukari. "Any problems?"

"Actually they just stopped it."

"What's wrong?"

"One of the gyroscopes lit up red. There doesn't seem to be a problem with the unit, so they think it's a sensor malfunction. We're probably looking at a thirty-minute delay."

"Roger that. Keep me posted."

"*Hoi*."

Problems like this happen all the time, thought Yukari. *Pathfinder was delayed two hours before it finally launched too.*

As she waited for the countdown to resume, Yukari went over the rest of the flight procedure.

Fully prepared for launch, the rocket stood twenty-one meters tall. The capsule containing Yukari was sixteen meters above the ground. The launch escape rockets were above the capsule, and below stretched the main booster, with two smaller solid rocket boosters attached to either side. All three would ignite to begin liftoff. The rocket would then slowly pick up speed as it rose and flew to the east.

For now, Yukari was responsible for making periodic reports to mission control and operating the emergency escape controls should the need arise. If it did, she would release the safety with her left hand and pull the escape lever. The first pull would separate the capsule from the main booster, the second would fire the launch escape rockets, propelling the capsule away from the launchpad. Then she would manually deploy the parachutes.

All the other controls were handled either by the onboard computer or remotely from mission control. The astronaut had no control over the firing of the boosters. Even if she wanted to, the G load during launch would be so high it would be hard to even reach the control panel.

The rocket would reach "max Q" roughly forty seconds after launch. Max Q was the point at which a rocket came under maximum aerodynamic stress. In Yukari's case, this would occur at an altitude of approximately ten thousand meters, with the rocket traveling faster than the speed of sound.

Two minutes ten seconds into the flight, the solid rocket boosters would separate. The main booster would continue its burn, and since the rocket would be considerably lighter without the weight of the two SRBs, the g-forces would climb as it accelerated.

At this point, the launch escape rockets were no longer needed, so they would be jettisoned as well. As the rocket grew lighter, it would achieve its maximum acceleration of 9 G. This was fully three times as high as the forces experienced by the space shuttle, but Yukari's time in the centrifuge had prepared her for it.

After six minutes eleven seconds, the main booster burn would be complete. The capsule would separate from the booster's empty husk and begin free flight at an altitude of 185 kilometers, traveling at 7.58 kilometers per second—orbital velocity.

The orbital thrusters at the rear of the capsule would then propel it into a circular orbit at an altitude of 210 kilometers. Forty-five minutes later the thrusters would briefly fire once more. All the while the spacecraft would be feeding telemetry to mission control, supplemented by Yukari's own observations.

The capsule would orbit the earth four times in the span of six hours. Halfway through its final orbit, the thrusters would fire a retrograde burn to break orbit. Slowly, the capsule would begin to descend, and at an altitude of approximately 130 kilometers, it would reenter the atmosphere.

During reentry, communications with the ground would be temporarily cut off. The onboard computer controlled the timing of the retrograde burn, the angle of reentry, and the attitude of the ship, but if there were a malfunction, Yukari would need to perform these manually.

When the capsule dropped below the speed of sound, the parachutes would open. The capsule would splash down at thirty-six kilometers per hour, and floats would deploy to keep the capsule above water.

The landing zone was a patch of ocean five hundred miles north of Maltide. There would be recovery helicopters and ships there waiting, but if the capsule came down off target, it could take time for them to reach the capsule. The capsule would be drifting during the search, making it difficult to find.

Yukari would be flying a nearly perfect equatorial orbit, so there was little danger of her landing somewhere she would freeze to death, barring the unlikely event of her landing on Mount Kilimanjaro or the mountains of New Guinea.

Yukari shook the thought from her head.

Don't even think about it. Everything will be fine.

She looked at her watch. It was already seven thirty. She flicked on the comm switch. "Mission control, *Tampopo*. Any update on our schedule?"

"We should have something for you soon, Yukari."

"Is it serious?"

"The gyroscope seems fine. They're telling me there's a problem with the sensor's data correction."

"We still looking at a thirty-minute delay?"

"For now."

"Roger that."

At 8:00 AM, Yukari had been in the capsule for two and a half hours.

"Mission control, *Tampopo*. How's it looking?"

"They're discussing options now. Hang on a sec." Two minutes passed. "Turn off main power and leave the capsule, Yukari."

"What?"

"They're delaying the launch until tomorrow."

"Uh, roger that."

When Yukari stepped out of the car in front of the command center, the press was waiting.

"How do you feel, Yukari?" asked a reporter.

"This sort of thing happens," said Yukari, her voice calm.

"Has the delay shaken your faith in the rocket?"

"Not at all. It just shows how thoroughly they're checking things."

[ACT 4]

IT WAS 7:20 AM the following morning.

A heavy metallic thud reverberated through the rocket. Yukari nodded to herself.

"Mission control, *Tampopo*. We have successful gantry separation."

"*Hoi*. Separation successful. We'll be performing final LOX pressurization in a moment."

"Roger that. Good luck."

Yukari watched the clock on the control panel as she listened for the sound of the pressurization equipment outside the rocket. *Forty minutes to go.* Once the flight started, it would all be over in six hours—not much longer than it would take her to fly back to Japan. Yukari would have plenty to brag about when she got back; she would have literally traveled the four corners of the globe.

That she had stumbled into being an astronaut did bother her, however. Would she continue the lies she had told the media? Not that there wasn't some truth to it—who hadn't thought about flying on a space shuttle at least once when they were a kid?

Yukari glanced at the control panel. It was an ugly thing—whoever designed it hadn't put much effort into the aesthetics. But if it got her back in one piece, she was willing to forgive it its flaws.

In a few years, maybe she would even come back to visit the islands, slip into the capsule, and wax nostalgic about all she had gone through in it—if she even still fit inside, which was doubtful.

Yukari couldn't control her height, but she was determined to not put on any weight. They had promised to let her keep her suit after the mission, but if she put on even a couple of kilograms, it would no longer fit. Not that she had any intention of wearing it in public.

But what if they made her go on television in the suit? Yukari didn't care for that idea at all. She could stand going to elementary schools, giving speeches about how beautiful the earth is, and being swarmed by little kids just as Mamoru Mohri, the first Japanese astronaut, had been. Yukari wondered what the earth would look like from space. Was it really that beautiful? They said going into space changed your perspective on life forever. In one hour, Yukari would see for herself.

She was starting to get excited. This was really happening. Yukari gave a shout of joy.

Matsuri came over the speakers. "*Hoi*. We've hit a little problem, Yukari."

Yukari came crashing back to reality. "What is it?"

"It looks like a liquid oxygen leak. One of the two sensors is showing a problem. They don't think it's anything serious, but they want you to power down the capsule and get out."

"Hang on. If it's not serious, why can't I just wait it out in here?"

"Director Nasuda wants to play it safe, just in case. Come on down."

"If I leave now, they'll have to restart the countdown, we'll miss the launch window, and the whole thing will be delayed. Again."

"The delay is already official. The fun will have to wait for tomorrow."

Yukari started to object, but she knew it was pointless.

"Roger that."

With her helmet tucked under one arm, Yukari stepped out of the elevator and walked down the ramp at the base of the launchpad. She stepped into the waiting Humvee and rode to the command center in silence. When they arrived, reporters thronged around her as she stepped out of the car.

"How does it feel to have your launch delayed again?" asked one of the journalists.

"I'm used to it," said Yukari, her irritation thinly veiled.

"The rocket seems to be having one problem after another. Has this shaken your faith in the safety of your launch?"

"Not at all."

"Some people are saying that safety has been sacrificed for the sake of weight and cost."

"No comment."

"Don't you find it troubling that the test launch went so smoothly, while your own rocket has been plagued with problems?"

Yukari glared at the reporter. "If there's something you want to say, say it."

"I'm just—that is, I was only asking."

"Then why don't you try 'asking' Chief Engineer Mukai?" Yukari turned and strode into the command center.

[ACT 5]

"PACING BACK AND forth like that is only going to make you hungry," said Matsuri, peering down from the top bunk. "You should try and get some sleep. Tomorrow's a big day."

"Is it?" Yukari shot back. "You know the launch will just be delayed again."

"Getting upset about it will stir up angry spirits, Yukari. Maybe I should use some magic to ward them off and get some good spirits to protect you."

"I don't need any more magic."

"I won't charge you or anything."

"Thanks, but no thanks." Yukari stopped pacing and leaned against the wall. "I don't want some creepy meddling spirits watching over me. I made it through my high school exams on my own. I can make it through this."

"*Hoi.* Whatever you say, Yukari." Matsuri was relieved to see Yukari still had some fight in her. "You don't have to sleep if you don't want to, but can we turn out the lights and go to bed?"

"Okay."

As Yukari was busy not falling asleep, Mukai was in a room beneath the launchpad pulling his fifth consecutive all-nighter.

"Come on, Satsuki, I'm desperate," pleaded Mukai.

"Absolutely not. A stimulant will only make you more tired later."

"I just have to make it till morning. This is it, I can feel it."

"And what if there's another delay?"

"That's why I need to stay awake—to make sure there isn't."

"Sorry. You'll have to make do with the IV."

"I don't have two hours to sit through an IV."

Satsuki looked at Mukai. His ashen features spoke of utter exhaustion. "Fine," she said, sighing. "Sit down."

"You're a lifesaver."

Satsuki took a syringe from her breast pocket and jabbed Mukai in the arm with five milligrams of Dormicum.

"That should help you relax."

"Huh? Relax? I don't have time to...relax..." Mukai's chin came to rest on his chest.

"Everyone knows their job. They'll do just fine without you," said Satsuki. Mukai was already sound asleep. "It's a shame you'll have to miss the launch."

[ACT 6]

DECEMBER 29, 8:50 AM

YUKARI HAD ALREADY been in the capsule for three hours and twenty minutes, and the countdown was still on hold.

"I think I deserve an explanation. 'We have doubts about the gyroscopes' isn't going to cut it," said Yukari.

"Just try and hang in there a little longer."

"I want explanations, not platitudes. Put Mukai on."

"Mukai's sleeping, but Director Nasuda is here. Hang on a sec."

"We've been analyzing the telemetry from Pathfinder, and we found some unexpected vibrations during launch," said Director Nasuda. "We don't think it's coming from an external source—it could be the booster itself."

"It didn't seem to have any trouble getting into orbit."

"That could have been sheer luck. This is a critical component we're dealing with here. With Mukai out of commission, I'd rather err on the side of caution."

"If we let every little thing scare us, we'll never launch."

"We still have two days before the deadline. There's no rush."

"What about what this is putting me through? I can let two scrubbed launches slide, but three? Forget it!"

"You were the one clamoring for us not to cut corners. This isn't the time to throw caution to the wind."

"If something goes wrong, I can always fire the escape rockets."

"The rocket could break up before you have time to react. No, we've done all we can today. Come on down."

Yukari didn't answer.

"Do you read me, Yukari?"

"I'm *not* leaving this capsule." Her voice was a low growl.

"That's an order, Yukari."

"If you want me down, I'm bringing the capsule with me."

"What do you mean?"

"I'll fire the emergency escape rockets. I may not have control over the boosters, but from the capsule up, this is *my* ship."

"This isn't funny."

"Do you hear me laughing?" Yukari's voice was ice. "You can't call someone the pilot and then ignore them when it comes time to fly. And what good is a rocket you can't fly when you want to? Restart the countdown. *Now.*"

Yukari knew how to hit Nasuda where it hurt.

"Let me think it over."

"You've got one minute. If the countdown isn't started by then, the capsule and I are both coming down."

"Understood."

Fifty-six seconds later, Matsuri's voice came through the speakers. "*Hoi*, Yukari. They've given us the go sign. The countdown will resume at T-minus five minutes."

"Now we're talkin'!"

At once, signs of life returned to the launchpad. A mechanical symphony of sounds reverberated in the cockpit.

"Flight control data check," said Matsuri.

"Control data nominal."

"Chronometer check."

"Chronometer is running."

"Set APU standby switch to on."

"APU standby on."

T-minus three minutes.

"Access arm retracted. Commencing SSWS flood procedure. Increase comm volume by two."

"Comm volume plus two," confirmed Yukari.

T-minus two minutes.

"Liquid oxygen release valves sealed. LOX at launch pressure."

"All capsule systems nominal."

T-minus one minute.

"Switching to internal power."

"Internal power nominal."

T-minus twenty seconds.

"Main booster APU start," said Matsuri.

"APU start confirmed. I can hear it."

T-minus fourteen seconds.

"Last chance to cancel, Yukari."

"Do it and die."

"*Hoi.* T-minus ten...nine...eight...seven. Main booster ignition. Four...three...two...one. SRB ignition."

The mission event timer went positive. The rocket shuddered as it lurched skyward.

"We have liftoff. *Tampopo* has cleared the launch tower."

Yukari felt as though she were sitting in a swing. There were hardly any g-forces.

"Vibration minimal," reported Yukari. "It's a smooth launch."

On the screen in the control room, the rocket rose into the sky atop a brilliant pillar of light. A ripple of applause erupted as Yukari's voice echoed through the room, but it soon died down. They had only passed the first step.

"Roll complete. We're on course," said Kinoshita, reading through the flight procedure. "Matsuri, inform Yukari she's about to enter max Q."

"*Hoi.* Yukari, prepare for max Q."

"Roger. I'm at 3.6 G now. The vibration is ramping up. All instruments read nominal."

"Entering max Q."

"Whoa...She's pitching pretty heavily. Altitude ten kilometers. Instruments nominal."

Yukari's breathing was uneven.

"She's fine," said Satsuki. "Pulse and respiration are still in the green." No one knew Yukari's limits better.

"Mission control, *Tampopo*. I think we're past max Q. All systems normal."

"*Hoi*, Yukari. You're doing great."

"The sky is getting dark. I still can't see any stars, but it's a deep navy blue now."

"Roger that, Yukari."

"Altitude sixty kilometers, 3.9 G. Instruments nominal."

"Solid rocket booster burn complete. Initiating separation sequence."

"SRB separation confirmed. I wonder if I can see them on the screen."

"They'll already be out of your field of view," said Kinoshita.

"Roger that. I can see the horizon curving outside the porthole now. There's an island ahead and to starboard. This all looks a lot more real than in the simulator."

That comment elicited a few smiles in the control room.

Kinoshita, however, remained all business. "*Tampopo*, this is mission control. Do you really see an island through the porthole?"

"Affirmative. One big island, clear as can be. I can even make out bits of reef to the left of it. Probably one of the Gilbert Islands."

"Copy that. How does the curvature of the horizon compare with the simulator?"

"Pretty much the same."

Kinoshita switched off the mike and looked at the rocket's position on the screen. "The Gilbert Islands should be just a few dots from where she is. Anything from our tracking stations?"

"We've already lost her. We'll have to wait for Christmas Island to pick her up," said one of the flight controllers.

"The telemetry looks good. Current altitude 160 kilometers," said the orbital guidance controller.

Kinoshita turned to Director Nasuda. "She might be off course. Do we want to abort?"

"Not yet," answered Nasuda. "Let's give it some time."

"*Hoi.* If we're going to abort, it has to be soon. The escape rockets will separate soon."

"We're not aborting," said Nasuda.

"If the gyroscopes are lying to us, she could be in real danger," said Kinoshita.

"Yukari's reports confirm the altitude. At this point it's safer to let her get in one orbit than scramble to abort."

Yukari's voice crackled over the speakers. "Mission control, *Tampopo*. Emergency rockets jettisoned. I could see the flash when they fired."

"*Hoi.* Roger that, Yukari. Main booster cutoff in three minutes forty seconds."

"Copy." There was a pause before Yukari's next transmission. "Mission control...*Tampopo*." Her voice was strained. "Acceleration at 6.1 G and climbing. She's shaking quite a bit...but not as bad as max Q. All instruments nominal."

"Just twenty more seconds, Yukari."

"Roger. Whoa, I feel light now! No acceleration. My arms are floating. Main booster separation confirmed. Attitude nominal."

"Keep your arms on the armrests, Yukari. Prepare for OMS burn."

"Roger—there it is!" The rumble of the orbital maneuvering system carried over Yukari's open mike. "OMS burn complete. It's quiet now—unbelievably quiet. Altitude 204 kilometers. Am I in orbit?"

"*Hoi.* Congratulations, Yukari. We're all smiles down here. How does the earth look? Anything you want to say?"

"The clouds are amazing—I wish I had a bigger window."

"Good job, Yukari," said Kinoshita. He was looking at the orbital display. "You should be in range of Christmas Island."

He called the tracking center. "This is Solomon mission control. Could you report *Tampopo*'s position?"

"We don't have *Tampopo* at this time."

"Check again."

A brief pause. "Confirmed. Radar is operational, but we're not tracking anything."

"Roger that. Let us know the minute you pick anything up." Kinoshita switched his transmitter to Yukari. "*Tampopo*, this is mission control. What do you see out the porthole?"

"The island from before is at the top of the window—wait, I think it's at the bottom. There's a different island up ahead. That's weird, I didn't think Christmas Island was that big."

"What does the island look like?"

"There are some tall mountains on the right, and it's narrower in the middle. It's so big—"Yukari fell silent. "Is that New Zealand? Why am I going south?"

No one spoke in the control room. They didn't have an answer for her.

In the Taliho village, the people gathered in the square gazed up at the sky. The "fireworks" had vanished from sight.

"Today's the twenty-ninth," muttered the chief. "The curse won't hurt anything...will it?"

CHAPTER VIII

MEDDLING SPIRITS

[ACT 1]

IN THE DARKENED cockpit, Yukari stared at the projection on the screen, a distorted image of the earth captured through the spacecraft's fish-eye lens. Far below her, the shadow of dusk settled over the earth.

Arcs of giant clouds burned red along a front, their peaks casting long shadows behind them. A thin layer of clouds drifted below like delicate crepes. Beyond the borders of the clouds extended a vast expanse of indigo ocean. White dots peppered the water, but Yukari couldn't be sure whether they were clouds or the caps of the waves.

"The water looks cold," muttered Yukari. These were not the warm waters of the atolls she had grown accustomed to. In the course of the twenty-five minutes she had been traveling over the South Pacific, the color of the water beneath her had steadily changed.

"You have an altitude reading for us yet?" asked Kinoshita. He had asked Yukari to measure her altitude using an onboard visual navigation system.

Yukari snapped out of her reverie. "Getting to it now." She aligned her scope with the curve of the horizon and read the measurements on the screen. It was a process one might have found on an ancient seafaring ship, only earth and sky were reversed. "Altitude 194 kilometers. Speed...7.8 kilometers per second."

"Sounds like you're in a stable orbit," said Kinoshita, the relief plain in his voice. Since *Tampopo* had reached orbital velocity, at least they didn't need to worry about her dropping out of the sky anytime soon.

"I'm approaching land now. South America, I think."

"Let's see if we can narrow that down. Check it against your map."

Yukari turned to the map in her operations manual and compared it with the image on the screen. An intricate coastline rolled toward her. Tendrils of murky water snaked their way toward a shore tinged with reddish brown.

"Hmm. I think I'm at fifty-one degrees south latitude—Puerto Montt in Chile. Passing over it now, MET reads twenty-seven minutes, fourteen seconds."

"Copy that. We'll start working on a plan to get you back."

"Have you figured out what went wrong yet? I'm dying to find out how I ended up in this whacked-out orbit."

"We're not sure yet," answered Kinoshita. There was a one-second interval between transmission and reception now. "Even if there was a problem with the gyroscope, that doesn't explain why our optical tracking lost you. As for why you're off course—and where the energy to make up for the energy lost putting you in an inclined orbit came from—we don't know. For now it's best to accept the fact and move on."

"Oh, I've accepted it." Yukari pursed her lips but said nothing more. What more could she say? After all, she was the one who had insisted on launching. If the problem during the launch was still a mystery, she had no one to blame but herself.

As far as Yukari was concerned, the entire program was dangerous, wasteful, self-serving—in general, a blight on the Solomon Islands. Nevertheless, she would feel bad if it were canceled because of her. At least they had put someone in orbit before the Department of Economic Planning's deadline expired. If Yukari could manage a safe splashdown, the base on the Solomons and the program would continue.

Since 70 percent of the earth was covered in water, the odds were on her side.

The main screen in the control room displayed a Mercator projection of the earth overlaid with a plot of *Tampopo*'s orbit. In the next hour, it would pass over the Brazilian highlands and the Atlantic, North Africa and Europe, Moscow and China, and finally the Philippines.

"I don't believe it—80 percent of this orbit takes her over land," said Director Nasuda with a tired sigh.

"This pass is no good," agreed Kinoshita. "The Philippines and New Guinea have too many islands, and after that we're into the Gold Coast. One mistake and we'd bring her down on land."

"And if our timing is off, she could end up below the fortieth parallel. She wouldn't last long in water that cold."

"Then we have to bring her down on her third orbit. Do a reentry burn over Sri Lanka for a splashdown to the south of the Cocos Islands."

Nasuda nodded. "It's an Australian territory, so there should be a naval base. We can probably get them to assemble a recovery team." Director Nasuda lifted a phone and started speaking to someone in English.

Kinoshita turned to Matsuri. "Tell Yukari we're planning on bringing her back on the third orbit."

"*Hoi*. Mission control to *Tampopo*. Yukari, we have a new reentry plan for you."

"When and where?"

"On your third orbit, with reentry over Sri Lanka and splash-down near the Cocos Islands in the Indian Ocean."

"The Cocos Islands? Never heard of 'em."

"It's a nice place. When I was little, the whole village went there by canoe."

"You're pulling my leg."

"The Taliho don't pull legs."

"All right, if you say so. Now what? I have three hours to kill."

"Don't worry, Yukari. We're going to be busy checking systems and practicing your attitude maneuvers. And since your gyroscopes are unreliable, we'll need you to make some navigational observations too."

"Roger that."

[ACT 2]

YUKARI CHECKED THE cabin pressure and carefully lifted the visor on her helmet. The cockpit smelled of rubber insulation. The whir of the ventilation fan and the hum of the electrical inverter were the only sounds that intruded on the eerie silence in the capsule.

"Mission control, this is *Tampopo*. I'm preparing to engage manual attitude control."

"*Hoi.* Copy that."

Yukari flipped the switch to enable manual control, grasped the control stick with her right hand, and released the safety.

"Starboard roll."

Yukari tilted the stick gently to the right.

Click.

A magnetic valve behind her opened. The thruster itself made no sound. The attitude indicator on the control panel began to spin.

"Roll rate, twenty degrees per second."

There was another *click* as Yukari returned the stick to the neutral position. The capsule stopped moving at once.

"Roll rate, zero. Easier than a video game."

"We want you to look outside to confirm you've stopped moving, Yukari."

"I can see the moon through the window. As steady as if it was hanging on a wall. It looks like a shining silver platter."

"It must be beautiful."

"You can see for yourself on the next flight."

"That's right!"

Yukari proceeded to test the manual controls on each of the three major axes of the ship. Everything checked out.

"Looks like the onboard gyroscopes are working fine. The jinx must have been on the booster," remarked Yukari.

"Oh no!" screamed Matsuri.

"What? What is it?"

"I'm so sorry, Yukari. I did something really, really stupid."

"*What?*"

"I forgot to tell Mom and Dad that the launch was delayed. I told them not to put a curse on the rockets going up on the twenty-seventh, but I never said anything about the launch today."

"That's it?" Yukari breathed a sigh of relief.

"What do you mean, 'that's it'? This is terrible! You don't know how powerful evil spirits can be." There was dead certainty in Matsuri's voice.

"But the rocket didn't blow up or anything. The orbit's just a little off, that's all."

"We can't let down our guard, Yukari. There are still evil spirits with you. It will only get worse from—"

A voice in the control room cut her off. "That's enough of that, Matsuri." The transmission went silent.

Yukari smiled to herself. "Believe in spirits all you want. I'm putting my faith in science. The attitude controls are working, so if we can do the deorbit burn and the parachutes open like they're supposed to, we're home free. Trust me, everything is going to be just fi—"

A violent jolt rocked the ship. Yukari screamed. She opened her eyes and saw the attitude indicator spinning wildly.

"Mission control, *Tampopo*." Yukari's voice was shaking. "We have a situation up here. Something shook the ship, and the capsule is spinning out of control. I've got an alarm on oxidation tank two—it's leaking. Other systems are—"

Kinoshita's voice came over the radio. "Close your visor and check the cabin pressure."

"Roger that. My visor is closed. Cabin pressure is normal. The B-39 control valve is lighting up red."

"Check your oxygen supply. If there's a problem, I want you to put on your emergency backpack."

"Oxygen supply reads normal." Yukari forced herself to breathe normally as she checked her instruments. "Cabin temperature and electric voltage are nominal. Life support systems all check out. Roll rate 314 degrees per second. Pitch rate 140 degrees."

"How's that oxidation tank?"

"Pressure is at zero. Must be empty."

"I don't want you to touch the attitude controls yet—it might trigger an explosion. As long as you have your number one tank, you're not in any danger. We can still bring you home."

"Copy that—Aiieee!"

"What is it?"

Yukari was about to report seeing sparks dancing outside the ship, but then she stopped herself. She had seen this in the videos they watched in class.

"I see 'fireflies' outside the window. Thousands of particles sparkling outside the ship. They're thinning out now."

"Probably the fluid from the oxidation tank. Do you see anything else?"

Yukari peered out the window. The capsule was still spinning, making it difficult.

"Uh-oh. I see something—something big. It looks like debris."

"Describe it."

"There's a long white piece—like tape or a cable or something. There's also something square, like a brick. It's black—I can't see it anymore."

"Continue your observations of the craft, inside and out. We'll be analyzing the telemetry."

"Um, Kinoshita? That black thing..." Fear had crept into Yukari's voice. "It looked like a heat shield tile."

It was three seconds before Kinoshita replied. "The tiles are diamond shaped, with a slight curve."

"That sounds right, but I didn't get a good look. I can't think of anything else it might have been."

If even one of the reinforced carbon tiles had become dislodged, reentry would be impossible—a simple fact known to everyone in the program, Yukari included.

"This doesn't look good...Do you know what happened?"

"That's what we're going to figure out. We have to take this one step at a time."

"I know, it's just..."

"Stay calm, Yukari."

"I am calm!"

"Oh? Your vital signs tell a different story."

"Huh?" Yukari's eyes went immediately to the heart-rate monitor. It was over 120 beats per minute. "Did Satsuki put the medical feed up on the screen?"

"I did," said Satsuki, her voice filling Yukari's helmet. "And if you want me to pull it down, you need to take some nice, deep breaths and relax." It was the first time Yukari had heard Satsuki's voice since the launch.

"I will, just shut it down! Or else I'm gonna rip the cables off myself."

"There, that's better." There was a smile behind Satsuki's words. "I think your body likes being angry, Yukari."

Yukari had played right into Satsuki's hands, which only upset her more.

"When you have some answers down there, I want to hear them. I'm the *captain*, remember? This whole thing caught me a little off guard, but I've got it together now. I can handle this. *Tampopo*, over and out."

Despite her brave words, the realization that she might not live through this had been kindled in the back of her mind. She would have to will herself to overcome her fear. It was the only way, and she knew it.

[ACT 3]

"IMPOSSIBLE!" SHOUTED MUKAI. They had woken him after four hours of sleep to break the news to him. "The designers would have taken the possibility of a tank overload into consideration. This isn't Apollo or Mars Observer—there's no way that tank could have ruptured on its own."

"All right," said Director Nasuda, folding his arms. "Space debris then."

There were countless pieces of trash in orbit around the earth, most of them little larger than specks of dust. But all of them traveled at speeds faster than a bullet fired from a rifle, each one a small, man-made satellite.

"The odds of an on-orbit impact with debris capable of crippling the ship are practically zero. Unless..." Matsuri's evil spirits came unbidden to Director Nasuda's thoughts, but he stopped short of blaming them.

Matsuri sat at her station, mouth agape, eyes vacant.

"Tank number two is here." Mukai indicated the tank on a diagram of the spacecraft. "This sausage-shaped object wrapped around the outside of the engine. Based on the location of the damaged valve, the debris must have impacted the side at an angle, piercing the tank and the heat shield."

"How do we fix it?" asked Director Nasuda.

Mukai started to speak, then paused again before answering. "I don't know if we can. Even assuming we could recover the tile, there's no way to reattach it to the hull."

"We might be able to use the adhesive in the space suit's repair kit," interjected Motoko. "It's good up to three hundred degrees."

"No, if the damage was bad enough to rip off a tile, the surface underneath will be a mess. Like a piece of paper with a hole punched through it."

"In light of the circumstances, I think it's worth a look," said Kinoshita. "We have to send Yukari out there to see what we're dealing with."

"In that suit? It's too dangerous," said Satsuki. "It was designed for use inside a spacecraft. It may be airtight, but it doesn't afford any protection against space debris or solar radiation."

"Then we'll only send her out while she's on the night side of the earth. And if somehow she does get caught on the day side, she can take shelter in the shade of the spacecraft. We can make this work."

"This is what manned spaceflight is all about!" crowed Director Nasuda. "We have eight hours. Time to pull out all the stops."

"You're enjoying this," said Satsuki.

The public relations officer entered the control room and approached Director Nasuda. "The press is going crazy. They want to know why the spacecraft is off its orbital flight plan and what we plan to do about it."

"We have nothing to hide," said Director Nasuda. "Get back out there and tell them the truth—*all* of it."

A minute later, it was headline news throughout the world.

[ACT 4]

"OUTSIDE? REALLY?"

"That's right. I know we didn't plan for an EVA, and your training for this is inadequate, but—"

"No, I'm in!" Yukari jumped at the opportunity. It beat twiddling her thumbs waiting for something to happen.

Yukari removed the emergency backpack from its storage place behind the seat and checked the airtight seal on her helmet. The backpack would provide an independent source of oxygen and power for up to an hour.

Next order of business was stopping the capsule from spinning. Yukari switched attitude control to manual and grasped the stick in her right hand. "Don't blow up..." she muttered. Watching the attitude indicator as she worked, she fired reaction thrusters to stabilize the capsule one axis at a time. The capsule handled as it had before, flawlessly.

With the capsule's spinning under control, Yukari followed instructions from the ground to reorient the spacecraft.

"Mission control, *Tampopo*. The capsule is in position."

"All right, now we want you to depressurize the cabin. Look for a handle on your right. It should have a red tag on it."

"I have it."

"Is your visor secured?"

"Affirmative."

Yukari removed the tag and rotated the handle. There was no sound, but the needle on the cabin-pressure dial began to move.

"Cabin depressurizing—it's getting cold."

"That should pass in a moment. Why don't you go ahead and attach your tether."

"Roger that."

A few minutes later, the interior of the ship was a vacuum. Yukari fired the thrusters again to compensate for the spin generated by the release of the air.

"Mission control, *Tampopo*. I'm preparing to open the hatch."

"Copy that. You are on the night side of the earth and will remain there for the next twenty minutes. Make sure you're back inside that capsule by then."

Yukari reached up and opened the hatch. A black square like the maw of a cave loomed above her. She released her harness and pulled on the edge of the hatch with her right hand. Yukari drifted upward.

A moment later, her upper body was outside the capsule. Her eyes went immediately to what appeared to be gas leaking from the bow of the spacecraft.

"There's something coming from the nose—" Yukari began, before realizing what it was she was seeing. It was the Milky Way, and for the first time she understood how it had earned the name.

A ruby red star glowed beside the Milky Way, and nearby was a tidy row of three brilliant stars.

"Orion...When was the last time I saw that?"

Seen from Maltide, Orion lay in the northern sky, just past the zenith, only inverted left to right from the way Yukari had grown up seeing it. The orientation of the capsule just happened to mimic the horizon near Japan, making Orion appear as Yukari remembered.

The stars were huge, brilliant—and none of them twinkled as they did on Earth. Yukari decided to test her knowledge of the constellations she had been taught. Looking from Orion to the far bank of the Milky Way, she found the twin stars Castor and Pollux that dominated Gemini. A little farther away she spotted Procyon in Canis Minor. Sirius should lie just beyond, but the bow of the ship hid it from view.

"*Tampopo*, this is mission control. What is your status?" Kinoshita sounded impatient.

"Oh, sorry. The stars are just so beautiful."

"You only have fifteen minutes till dawn."

"Roger that." Yukari turned slowly until she was facing the tail of the ship. The engine was two meters to the aft behind the hatch, which rose from the ship like a sail. "My entire body is outside now. I'm holding on to the hatch. This feels a lot like the underwater training actually. I'm looking down at the earth—it's pitch black. Wait, I think I see some lights. Where am I?"

"You're over the top of the Italian peninsula. You're about to pass to the south of Moscow, and then you'll be over the Tian Shan Mountains." Kinoshita stopped himself. "You need to be working on getting that floodlight turned on so you can examine the ship."

"Roger that, I'm on it."

Yukari switched on the light attached to her shoulder harness. The familiar surface of the capsule drifted in the circle of light.

"I don't see any problems—Wait!"

"What is it?"

"There's a hole on the starboard aft, just beneath the doors for the floats. It's about ten centimeters in diameter, with jagged edges."

"That's pretty much what we expected. Try and get a closer look at the heat shield. Be careful not to let your suit or the tether brush up against any of the damaged areas."

"Roger."

Grabbing on to projections on the surface of the ship, Yukari propelled herself forward using only her arms. It looked as though she were doing a handstand, but of course she was lighter than a feather.

Yukari reached the rear of the ship. The heat shield covering the tail was composed of neat rows of tiles arranged into a curved pancake shape. At its center was a small hole, out of which protruded the orbital maneuvering system engine nozzle and its protective door. Yukari maneuvered herself to the edge of the heat shield and directed her light on the tiles—and there it was.

"I've located the damage to the heat shield. It's by the OMS. There are two tiles missing, and the surrounding area is raised."

"What does it look like underneath the tiles?"

"The honeycomb mesh is torn to bits."

"Copy." A short pause. "If you had the tiles, do you think you could get them back in place?"

"Negative. The base is too uneven. It's about three centimeters higher than the surrounding surface, and there are cracks radiating from the center." Yukari reported her observations without emotion.

The damage she was seeing meant death for her, but somehow she remained calm—the fear would come later.

"Understood," said Kinoshita. "Go on and get back inside." His voice betrayed no trace of emotion.

[ACT 5]

DIRECTOR NASUDA HUNG up the phone. "The soonest they can have a shuttle up is four days—two weeks for a Soyuz. Nothing but inflexible, hulking leviathans."

Matsuri sprang to her feet. "*Hoi,* Mukai. How soon can our third rocket fly?"

"That's right—we have another rocket!"

The SSA had prepared three LS-5A boosters for this mission: Pathfinder, *Tampopo,* and a third still on its side in the VAB waiting to be assembled.

Mukai ran the numbers through his head. "Forty...no, twenty-four hours should do it."

"But the capsule will only hold one person," said Director Nasuda. "We can't use it to perform a rescue."

"Sure we can," said Matsuri. "We just have to launch it empty for a rendezvous with Yukari."

"It might work, but we don't have twenty-four hours. Yukari's life support will only last another eight—maybe twelve if we're careful."

"But she could use the liquid oxygen for the fuel. She can do another space walk and—"

"Matsuri, even if Yukari had enough oxygen, we would need some way to scrub the carbon dioxide out of the air," said Satsuki.

Matsuri fell silent, her eyes filling with tears.

Kinoshita, who up until now had been staring at his terminal, raised his voice. "These spirits of yours, Matsuri. They enjoy playing pranks, do they?"

"*Hoi.* Evils spirits love pranks. Sometimes they can even kill people."

Everyone turned toward Kinoshita to see where he was going with this.

"Well, I don't know whether to call this coincidence or what, but—look at the screen."

The screen displayed *Tampopo*'s orbit, and beside it, a second sine wave.

"Kinoshita, is that what I think it is?" asked Director Nasuda.

"That's the Russian space station—Mir. Its orbit is going to cross *Tampopo*'s at almost the exact same time. It should pass about two hundred kilometers above *Tampopo* on the next orbit. We couldn't have matched up the orbits better if we tried."

"Maybe things are finally turning our way. But climbing another two hundred kilometers isn't going to be easy."

"I ran the calculations, and if we jettison the parachute system, it can be done. The capsule will be stranded in orbit, but we can save Yukari. Mir has a three-man Soyuz docked that can bring her home."

"It's all coming together," said Director Nasuda with a pump of his fist.

This would add an unscheduled orbital rendezvous to the unscheduled EVA they had just completed. It would be difficult for people outside of the aerospace community to understand, but to accomplish so much on their first manned flight would be nothing short of a miracle.

"But we can't bring her home in a Ruskie ship—that would label the whole mission a failure. Mukai, I want that third ship on a rendezvous with Mir, and I want it yesterday."

"You don't have to ask twice."

[ACT 6]

PROFITABILITY IN THE space business took more than the ability to reach orbit—you had to be able to make your way to a satellite or ship once you got there. *Tampopo* may have been small, but it could execute dramatic orbital changes, and that was its great advantage. Any number of *Tampopo*'s features had been pared back to reduce size and weight, but not her OMS engine—the engine that was going to boost her to Mir.

Yukari listened as Kinoshita went over the steps they were about to take.

"We only get one shot at this. Your first burn will be at perigee in thirty-seven minutes—that will put you in a Hohmann transfer orbit. Forty-four minutes later you'll perform another burn to align your vector with Mir. Do you copy?"

"Roger. Just like we learned in class."

"That's right. Things are going to get a little hectic. Matsuri's back with us. She'll be providing your ground support again."

"Copy that. You there, Matsuri? Everything's okay up here."

"*Hoi*, I'm here. We still need to be careful, Yukari. Stay sharp."

"I know, I know. So, where do you wanna start?"

"First we're going to jettison the parachute system, then we're going to program the sequencer. We need to check the clock and the engine too. It's a pretty long list."

"Copy that."

An hour and twenty minutes passed. The first burn came and went without incident. *Tampopo* had entered an elliptical orbit that would bring it within striking distance of Mir's own. Mir would be approaching from behind, and when it was just about to overtake *Tampopo*, Yukari would perform an apogee burn to match speed.

For now, Mir was nowhere in sight.

"So...what's going on? Should I radio to let them know I'm coming?"

"Actually, Yukari, the talks with the Russians are still a work in progress. They're worried about the possibility of a collision, so they haven't given *Tampopo* permission to approach yet."

"They...what?"

Yukari couldn't believe what she was hearing. Were they really going to negotiate over her life?

The idea wasn't as absurd as it first sounded. Granting docking rights to a foreign country was a big deal; if something went wrong, astronomical sums of money were on the line, not to mention lives. They only had one chance for *Tampopo* to make the rendezvous with Mir, so they had taken it, a leap of faith that she would be welcome when she got there. But there was a real possibility that she would be turned away at the door.

"You're approaching Mir according to plan," said Matsuri. "U.S. Space Command is tracking your position for us. You're currently seventy-four kilometers from Mir, and nine kilometers below."

"I should be in ship-to-ship communications range by now."

"*Hoi*, affirmative. Want to give it a try?"

"They speak English, don't they?"

"Only one way to find out."

"Here goes. Let's see if they're willing to sit on their hands while a teenage girl dies."

Yukari flipped through the operations manual and tuned her radio to the common frequency used by international spacecraft.

"Um, hello, Mir?" Yukari spoke in English. "This is *Tampopo* from SSA, Yukari Morita speaking. Over."

On her second attempt, a reply came in English. "This is Mir. We hear you loud and clear, SSA *Tampopo*." It was a man's voice, deep and resonating.

Yukari was ecstatic as she pressed the talk button. "This is *Tampopo*. I hear you loud and clear too. *Tampopo* can't make reentry. I was hoping you'd let me stay with you. Over."

"Mir to SSA *Tampopo*. TsUP mission control has informed us of your situation, but we have not yet received permission for you to dock."

Yukari realized it was now or never.

"So the Russians are just going to let a young girl die with the whole world watching?"

The Russian response came almost immediately. "Mir to SSA *Tampopo*. I want you to listen carefully to what I am going to tell you, Yukari. Cosmonauts, astronauts—we have all answered the same noble calling. As far as we are concerned, everyone on the ground can piss off."

Yukari couldn't have been more thrilled by what she had heard if it had been in her own native Japanese. In a place lonelier than any on Earth, she had forged a bond with another human being.

"Thank you, Mir. I'm glad we had the chance to meet like this. Oh, I still don't know your name, do I?"

"I am Oleg Kamanin. With me is my commander, Nikolai Belyayev."

"Just two of you?"

"Correct. We have been here six months. Nikolai is depressurizing and prebreathing to prepare so he can meet you outside the station. It will be two hours before he can go out. Can you wait until then?"

"Two hours is no problem. Life support should last another four."

"Copy that. TsUP told us your suit does not require prebreathing. This is true?"

"Of course. I thought that's how they all were."

"An amazing technology. This is good, but there will be other difficulties with docking. We will need to moor your vessel to the station with tethers, and our air lock is only large enough for one person at a time. Nikolai will help you tie up your ship and show you to the air lock."

"Roger. First I need to get there though. I still have seventy kilometers to go. How am I going to find you? I don't have much fuel, so I need to get it right the first time."

"This concerned us too, Yukari. That is why we already track you on radar. We have a good fix on your position. We will guide you to us."

"You're a lifesaver, Oleg."

Yukari didn't waste any time reporting her conversation with Mir to SSA mission control in the Solomons.

"I don't know what kind of progress you're making down there, but we have a game plan ready up here. I'm currently approaching Mir under their guidance. I'm at a relative distance of sixty-three kilometers, elevation minus four kilometers. I should reach Mir in twenty-four minutes."

Yukari spoke with absolute confidence. Oleg had said that astronauts of all nations answered to a noble calling, and she liked the sound of that. To this point, she had dutifully followed whatever instructions the ground had given her, but real astronauts relied on their own judgment, made their own decisions, and carried them out. It felt good to be in control.

"Mir is directly ahead—bright, it looks like Venus. I hope they have a shower onboard. I wouldn't mind a bite to eat either."

"Nice going, Yukari. Everybody's celebrating down here." Even Matsuri was having trouble containing her excitement.

"They should be. An astronaut who's never flown before doing an EVA and an on-orbit rendezvous in a one-manned spacecraft? This has to be some sort of record."

"*Hoi*. Director Nasuda's beside himself."

"NASA only lets their top astronauts do EVAs. When I get back, maybe I'll pay a visit to Houston and say hi."

[ACT 7]

FROM A DISTANCE of a few kilometers, Mir looked like a white cross. It was impossible to gauge distance in the vacuum of space, so it appeared to hang there like a key chain dangling just outside the window.

Tampopo performed her apogee burn and made her final approach, coming in one hundred meters above Mir.

As Yukari oriented the capsule vertically above the station, the earth swung into view, its orb dusted with snow-white clouds, followed by Mir itself, which had been hidden during the final leg of the approach.

"Wow, it's *big*." Yukari was awestruck.

Mir had grown considerably in the ten years since its launch. With its two Kvant modules, Kristall modules, and docked Soyuz, it was a massive structure reaching over forty meters in length.

Yukari wrung the last bit of thrust out of *Tampopo*'s engine to maneuver toward the end of Mir's Kristall-2 module, bringing the ship to a stop a few meters from the air lock.

"Mir, *Tampopo*. I'm in position."

"Beautiful approach, Yukari. You are a natural."

"Just doing my best." Yukari felt her cheeks redden. "Mir is pretty big. I feel like a fly on an elephant's tail."

Oleg laughed. "I like this expression. Let me tell you about our home while Nikolai prepares to go out. Can you see the window I am in?"

"Um, where?"

"Two meters past the air lock, in the middle of a tangle of equipment."

Yukari peered eagerly out of her capsule. She spotted a small round window surrounded by pipes and handholds—and in the window she saw Oleg. He was younger than she expected. His hair was wavy and blond. He had a slender face with chiseled features. In short, he was quite handsome.

"Do you see me?" asked Oleg.

"Yes, I see you. Can you see me?"

"Unfortunately it is too dark. I will have to wait."

"What about Nikolai? Can he talk with us?"

"He is prebreathing in his space suit now."

"You don't have radios in your space suits?"

"No, it is not that. He is a little quiet, that's all."

Yukari cocked her head. She had never heard of a quiet astronaut. If anything, the ability to communicate and work together was something to be prized in the space program.

"Well, he *is* Russian," Yukari said to herself. She had always harbored a little prejudice against Russians. "But he's also a professional astronaut—I guess I can trust him."

Two hours later, the round door of the air lock swung open to reveal a figure in a bulky space suit.

"This is Commander Nikolai Belyayev. I have exited the air lock. Do you read me, *Tampopo*?" He spoke in a husky baritone. Whatever his reason for not joining in their conversation sooner, it wasn't for a lack of English ability.

"I hear you loud and clear, Commander Belyayev."

"I'm going to throw you a tether. Get out of your ship."

"Roger."

Yukari opened the hatch and boosted herself halfway out of the ship. A gold visor concealed Nikolai's face. He tied a wrench to one end of the tether and threw it to Yukari. It sailed magically through the gap separating them, the tether trailing in an undulating wave. She caught the wrench and tied the tether to a handle on her now derelict craft.

"First we will take care of you. Oleg explained the workings of the air lock to you, yes?"

"He did."

"Pull yourself here along the tether. Once you are in the air lock, I will finish securing your ship."

"You don't need me to help?"

"It is a one-man job."

"Understood."

Nikolai was not the friendliest of people.

A little nervous, Yukari headed for the air lock.

CHAPTER IX

THE BLUE PLANET AWAITS

[ACT 1]

YUKARI HAD EXPECTED Mir's air lock to be something like
an elevator, but it more closely resembled a tube with a manholelike hatch on its far end. She entered feetfirst and closed the outer hatch above her head. With the flip of a switch, air began to
flood the chamber, and the needle on the pressure gauge started
to move. When the pressure in the air lock had equalized with the
pressure inside the space station, a green light came on. Yukari
then rotated a handle on the wall of the air lock to open the inner
hatch beneath her feet.

"I'm going to pull you in now. Let your muscles relax." Oleg
grabbed Yukari by the ankles and gave a gentle tug.

Yukari drifted into pure white light. The room she found herself in had neither ceiling nor floor. She was surrounded by pipes
and machinery. There was no clear 'up,' and it took Yukari a moment to adjust.

Grabbing hold of a handle on the wall, Yukari spun herself

around to face Oleg, who floated at an angle to her on his side. He was a head taller than Yukari, but the body beneath his blue coveralls bore the sleek build of a gymnast.

Oleg's wide, brown eyes were riveted on Yukari.

"Um..." What was proper etiquette for greeting someone in space?

Yukari decided to start by orienting herself the same direction as Oleg and removing her helmet. With the slightest spin of her body, her hair went every which way. Free of the 1 G in which it had been fixed, it gracefully spread out. Yukari extended both arms like a figure skater to stop herself from spinning. As she did, her hair danced as it recoiled into her shoulders and chest.

Without realizing it, Yukari burst into a smile. She had been unable to enjoy the full experience of microgravity in the confines of her capsule.

Oleg was transfixed. "At last we meet. Welcome aboard Mir," said Oleg, embracing Yukari in a bear hug.

"What? Hey!"

Oleg held Yukari nearly a minute before finally letting go, and his eyes soon settled back on her body. Yukari's skintight suit, a scant two millimeters thick, left precious little to the imagination.

"You are a vision," said Oleg.

Under the circumstances, Yukari was willing to forgive his behavior. Oleg and his commander had been alone aboard the station for over half a year, after all.

"It's, uh, nice to meet you. I can't thank you and Nikolai enough for letting me aboard." Yukari extended her hand.

The gesture seemed to restore Oleg to his senses. He took Yukari's hand and gave it a firm shake.

"It is our pleasure, Yukari. Come, let us go to the core module. It is small, so you should leave your helmet and backpack here."

The interior of the space station was chaotic. Air ducts and cables snaked everywhere, making the already tight, tunnel-like space feel even more cramped. Bits of random junk were entwined along the walls. The air was filled with the loud whine of fans, and the place smelled like a locker room in the middle of summer.

It had already been over a decade since they had put the first module into orbit. Various patch-up jobs and additions hadn't been able to hide the gradually deteriorating conditions inside. Originally planned as a new station, Mir 2 had floundered along with the Russian economy, eventually winding up as part of a larger international space station. Now construction on that international station had hit a roadblock, and there was no support for full-time astronauts on board—which meant they had to make do with Mir.

"If this had been the main air lock in the Kristall-2 module, we would have been able to fit your entire capsule inside," Oleg said as she was moving in. "But it has been broken for some time. Now we use only for storage."

Yukari was not inspired with confidence.

"Isn't that dangerous?"

"If something happens we can escape in the Soyuz."

A simplified version of the Soyuz remained docked at Mir at all times for use as an emergency escape vehicle.

Yukari peeled back a cloth cover held in place by bungee cords and went through a narrow, manholelike port into the core module. Past a pilot's chair, with its switchboard and monitor, she arrived at the living quarters. This room was about three meters across, with a boxy dining table and four backless chairs attached to one of the walls.

A curtain ran along one side of the module, with a small space like a changing room behind it. Inside she spotted a sleeping bag attached to the wall and a single round window.

"That is my *kayuta*. I let you use."

"Kayuta?"

"My berth. It is a bit narrow, but there is no place like home, yes?"

Yukari smiled. "That'd be great. Thank you."

The Kvant-1 module beyond the living space had formerly been a science lab but was now relegated to use as a toilet and storage. Beyond that was the port where the Soyuz would be docked.

"We don't have much time for chitchat, but there is a very important thing you need to know. I will get right to the point," Oleg said, considerately describing how to use the toilet facilities.

Yukari listened, appreciating the man's straightforward demeanor.

It turned out there was something like a large suction cup that handled both solid and liquid waste, sucking it away along with a quantity of air. It didn't seem all that difficult to use. Much to Yukari's relief, the station was equipped with female facilities.

Oleg left, and alone at last, Yukari used the washbasin—the design required her to stick her hands and face into a sealed compartment—and gave a deep sigh of relief. It had been nine hours since she'd last washed, and she really needed it. Being here felt like arriving at a hotel after a long journey. A little cramped, but cozy all the same.

Back in the living area she paused for a moment when she saw the two men seated there waiting for her. She would have come to a complete stop if she hadn't already been floating in their direction. It was hard to freeze on the spot in zero gravity.

So this was Commander Belyayev. Out of his suit, the bulky Russian looked more like a bear than a man. He had black hair, thick eyebrows, and sideburns on a square face. He was a bit older than Oleg—maybe in his mid-forties, she guessed.

"Yukari Morita reporting," she introduced herself. "Thanks for the help out there."

Nikolai glared at her for a moment and said simply, "Good morning."

Mir ran on Moscow time, which made it six in the morning.

Yukari swallowed. *Maybe he's grumpy in the morning? Or maybe his blood pressure's just low because he's been up here so long.*

Oleg glanced between the two of them and cleared his throat. "Welcome, Yukari, to our humble abode. Here, have a seat. You will want to tuck your toes under the handle there on the floor. It is breakfast time. I hope our food is to your liking."

She sat down next to Oleg in the seat indicated. It felt odd having to bend her legs to fit on the chair, but once she was seated the arrangement felt much more like a conventional table, and the two cosmonauts much more like family.

"Should be about ready!"

Oleg lifted up the table lid, revealing an electric heating unit inside, with pockets for small cans and small tubes along an outer ring that were cool to the touch.

She took the can offered to her and pulled the tab to open the lid, revealing a brownish, gloopy substance inside. Wincing, she took a whiff and was overpowered by an intense smell of garlic. "What the…"

"Beef stroganoff!"

She set the can aside and reached for one of the tubes, but when she opened the lid, the stench of garlic assailed her nostrils again.

"And this is?"

"Borscht! It is a Russian specialty."

Yukari shook her head. Considering the cost of transportation, this meal must have been insanely expensive. *I can't exactly refuse it*, she thought, watching as Nikolai began working the gloop in the can with his spoon.

A call from TsUP broke the uneasy silence in the cabin. Oleg answered. After speaking in Russian for a while, he turned to them and said, "Yukari, you have a call from Solomon mission control. I told them you were eating, but they insist."

"Oh, okay. I'll talk to them," she replied, hoping her relief wasn't too obvious. She looked around for a moment, wondering where to set her spoon. Nikolai pointed toward a small magnetic plate on one corner of the table. Nodding, Yukari let her spoon clamp on to the magnet. She unhooked herself from the floor handle with her toes and floated up toward the ceiling, turning as she went to face the wireless communicator set into the wall.

[ACT 2]

"GET READY, WE'RE going live."

Mission control was packed with Japanese television reporters. The man speaking to Yukari was a producer chosen to represent the group. Director Nasuda wanted to take full advantage of the media, so when the press corps made a request, he bent over backward to accommodate them.

"And here we go in three...two...one."

A burst of applause filled the control room as the grainy image from the Russian space station appeared on the main screen.

Yukari waved at the wide-angle lens. "How's it going down there? Can you see me?"

"*Hoi*, you look good, Yukari!" Matsuri was her usual chipper self.

"Everything up here is shipshape. We were right in the middle of a welcome party when you called."

"I hope you're getting something to eat. You can't work on an empty stomach."

"This Russian food though—gag me."

"What's it like?"

"You wouldn't believe—"

"Let me talk to her," interrupted Kinoshita. "Yukari, I want to go over our plans for getting you home."

"Sure, okay."

"Right now we're preparing the third ship for launch. Unfortunately, the orbiter won't be able to reach Mir by relying on remote commands alone. We're going to need to downlink data from Mir's docking radar to mission control here in the Solomons and uplink that to the orbiter to guide it in. Understood?"

"I think so. I don't know what it's going to take for Mir to do that though."

"Could you put their commander on?"

"Sure, hang on."

Nikolai appeared on the screen and began discussing the situation with Kinoshita in English.

The television producer leaned over and whispered to Director Nasuda. "This is no good. We need to get Yukari back on."

"Patience, patience," replied Nasuda with a winning smile. "It's not as though you have to break for commercial anytime soon."

"No, but if the audience loses interest—"

"Look, we haven't gotten a formal reply from the Russians yet, so we want to pave the way by getting in good with their commander. It'll just take a minute."

"Let's hope so. We've got *Catching Up with the Moritas* after this."

"I know, I know. Once we get this business out of the way, she's yours for as long as you like."

When this producer had learned that Yukari would be visiting Mir, he had had an award-winning idea. Mir was equipped with a camera and the ability to send and receive video in real time. What better way to cover a Morita family reunion?

He had set up the lines for the broadcast in record time, with links between Japan, the Solomon Islands, and TsUP mission control in Russia. In exchange for the use of their bandwidth, myriad television stations around the globe would gain the rights to air the program—it would be broadcast live throughout Asia, Africa,

North America, Europe, and Australia.

As Kinoshita wrapped up his conversation with Commander Belyayev, the producer whispered to Matsuri. "You're up, Matsuri. Break a leg."

"*Hoi*. Yukari, we have a special surprise for you—a video conference with your parents. People all over the world will be watching."

"What?"

The image split into two windows. Yukari's father, Hiroshi Morita, appeared on the screen.

"You're looking well, Yukari."

"Uh, hi, Dad. Are you in the village?"

"A camera crew came out and asked me to talk to you."

"Talk to me about what?"

"Oh, you know, see how you're feeling."

"Never better. What about you? You found a new chief to replace you yet? You *are* getting ready to go back to Japan, right?"

"Things are moving."

"You promised."

"A promise is a promise, Yukari, but—"

Hiroko Morita interrupted. The producer scrambled to get a third window showing Yukari's mother on the screen. Hiroko was in the living room of their home in Yokohama. "After all this trouble to become an astronaut, what's all the hurry to get home?"

"I thought you were on my side, Mom."

"You're just going to leave Matsuri there all by herself? Or did you plan on bringing her back to Japan with you?"

Matsuri appeared in a fourth window. "*Hoi*, I want to fly on a few missions before I decide."

"There, you see?"

"How do you like space, Yukari?" interrupted her father. "Is one trip going to be enough to get it out of your system?"

"I haven't had time to think about it. So far I've had my hands full with one emergency after another."

"And you pulled it off," said her mother. "Doesn't that make you feel proud?"

"A little, maybe."

"They still need Hiroshi in the village—why not stick with the program a little longer, brush up your skills?"

"But I *want* to go back to school! If I'm not back by next semester, they're going to hold me back a grade!"

"What's one year?"

"Aren't you worried at all?"

"About what?"

"I was almost killed!"

"There's danger everywhere," replied Hiroko. "Your dying in space is something I could come to terms with, but what if you were hit by a car in front of the house or you slipped on a bar of soap in the bathtub? It's a meaningless death like that that worries me."

"Which is exactly the problem."

"Morimori died from a snakebite," said Matsuri.

"That's right, she did, didn't she," said Hiroshi. "Such a waste..."

"Who's Morimori?" asked Yukari.

"Morimori was my daughter with...Tongua, I think it was."

"Ladies and gentlemen, this man can't even remember the names of the mothers of his children."

"Still can't get enough, eh, Hiroshi?" said Hiroko.

"It's hard for a leopard to change his spots," admitted her father.

"Tankuku drowned in the river," continued Matsuri. "Lapepe was kicked by a boar."

"And Kalengi ate some bad fish, as I recall."

"We lost a foreman at one of our construction sites," offered Hiroko. "A crane fell over in the wind—his brains were all over the place."

"Wind can sneak up on you like that."

"The trouble is when it blows intermittently—once harmonic vibration kicks in, it's all over."

"*Hoi*, you should have made an offering to the wind spirits."

"You're pretty superstitious for an astronaut," said Yukari.

"Don't be so hard on your sister, Yukari," said Hiroshi. "Even in Japan they don't break ground on a new building without a religious ceremony."

"Listen to your father, Yukari. Plenty of people take these things seriously."

"You two are certainly on the same page."

"We did know each other *before* the honeymoon, you know," said Hiroshi.

"But this is the first time we've talked in sixteen years," added Hiroko.

"Do you know anyone who's died, Yukari?" asked Matsuri.

"You really like this morbid stuff, don't you, Matsuri?"

"*Hoi!*"

"Well, let's see. There was a girl in school who got stung by a wasp."

"I remember that. Caused quite a stir at the PTA meeting," said Hiroko.

"We have wasps here too, don't we, Matsuri?"

And so it went. The producer, who had hoped for a teary reunion, was dumbfounded but powerless to stop it. The Morita family talked until Mir passed out of range.

[ACT 3]

YUKARI SPENT THE rest of the day answering calls from the media at Solomon mission control and throughout the world. She was in one interview or another right up until lights-out on Mir. By then she had been up more than twenty-four hours straight, and she was exhausted.

Yukari went to Oleg's kayuta and watched as he showed her how to use the sleeping bag. It made her feel like a bug in a cocoon, but in zero gravity there weren't many options.

"You looked very happy talking with your family," said Oleg.

Yukari's head was the only part of her body protruding from the sleeping bag. "Hmm, you think so?" She cocked her head. "I didn't feel particularly happy."

"But you were. During breakfast you were nervous. But after you spoke with family, you seem relaxed, at home."

"Really?"

Yukari had felt frustrated, annoyed, even angry...but happy?

The impromptu family reunion had caught her completely off guard. She had imagined their reunion would take place outside of customs at Narita Airport. Her father would be wearing a suit, and they would come walking out together, side by side, to find her mother waiting for them. There would be no teary spectacle, much to the dismay of the media thronging around them. The three of them would walk past the cameras and microphones with neither a nod nor a word, and they would go home together for the first time. And when they were home, they would talk about anything and everything.

Instead, the reunion had taken place via four-way satellite teleconference. On live television, they had started bickering back and forth almost as soon as they had opened their mouths, seemingly oblivious to the fact that Yukari was speaking to them from aboard a Russian space station. They had spoken their minds in front of the whole world.

"So that's what it feels like to be a family," she said in Japanese. Then, in English, "Do you have a family, Oleg?"

"Yes. Wife, but no children yet."

"Do you talk to your wife the way we talked today?"

"Sometimes, yes." Oleg seemed a little nervous.

Yukari decided to ask something that had been bothering her. "What about Nikolai? Does he have a family?"

"Wife and two children."

"He seems like he's in a bad mood. Did you two get in a fight or something?"

"With me? No. We get along well."

"Then with his family, maybe?"

"Hard to say."

"You live together. How can you not know?"

"We do our best not to intrude."

"Being up here for over half a year, don't you ever feel...unfulfilled?"

Oleg shook his head. "Only the chosen few can do our job. It is a great honor."

"I think I get it." Oleg had given Yukari a stock answer, but it had made something click. "So there *is* something different about real astronauts. Were you in the military?"

"Yes, I flew Sukhoi fighters in Khabarovsk. Nikolai was an upperclassman when I was at air force academy. Finally he was promoted to desk job, but he never gave up his dream of flying higher, faster. So he applied to be cosmonaut."

"A real go-getter."

"Nikolai is incredible man. But do not sell yourself short. You are real thing, Yukari."

"I don't know..."

"And so charming too."

"Thanks." Yukari smiled. "You don't know how happy you made me when you decided to let *Tampopo* dock."

"Do not mention it. No one knew how you must have felt better than we did."

"Thanks," she said again.

A wave of relief surged over her. She had washed up on the shores of a man-made island in space called Mir, and she was lucky to be here.

Her anxiety had held sleep at bay, and with it gone, she felt her eyelids grow heavy.

"Sorry, I can barely keep my eyes open."

"Sleep well, Yukari. Good night." Before Oleg had turned from the kayuta, Yukari was already fast asleep.

[ACT 4]

"IT'S LIGHTS OUT on Mir," announced Kinoshita, removing his headset.

"Maybe we should do the same," said Director Nasuda. "Good work, everyone."

Exhausted, the other controllers removed their headsets in unison, leaning back in their chairs and stretching as they did.

Kinoshita left his workstation and approached Director Nasuda. "That just leaves the third ship. If we can pull this off, we've got a mission for the history books."

"That we do. Did you find the problem with the gyroscope on the main booster?"

"One of the damper components wasn't up to spec. We've already finished repairs."

"Good. Hopefully that's the last trouble we'll have from Matsuri's 'evil spirits.'" Director Nasuda let out a long sigh.

Satsuki walked into the control room carrying a tray of coffee.

"Just what the doctor ordered," said Director Nasuda.

"Without any medical telemetry, *this* doctor had too much free time on her hands," said Satsuki.

"It's too bad. I'm sure you'd love to get some data of Yukari sleeping," said Kinoshita.

"She's probably sleeping like a baby. I doubt the data would be all that interesting," replied Satsuki. "Yukari really did great today though. She has courage and focus in spades."

"With a family like hers, she needs it."

"Do you think she'll really quit after this?" asked Director Na-suda, his face pained. "Yukari has rare talent. I don't know what she sees in going back to high school."

"She wants a normal life," said Kinoshita. "Two parents, friends that treat her like everyone else."

"She said as much, didn't she," Director Nasuda conceded.

Kinoshita smirked. "Normal may be harder for her than she thinks."

"Normal is overrated. Do you know how many kids these days are raised by single parents?"

"But it's important for her," Satsuki said. "We have to support her decision."

"You're right, of course," Director Nasuda said, fighting back a yawn. "I think I'm going to lie down. Any beds around here?"

"There are some cots in the break room in the training center."

Director Nasuda left the control room grumbling about how he used to be able to stay up for two nights in a row when he was younger.

[ACT 5]

YUKARI WOKE TO the sound of voices. She wasn't sure how long she had been asleep. One of the voices was raised, angry. Nikolai, she thought. It seemed as though Oleg were defending himself against some accusation, but she couldn't understand what they were saying.

The argument grew more heated. She heard a crash as two objects collided, followed by the sound of Oleg's voice, uncharacteristically high. Yukari couldn't sit still any longer. Whatever their reasons for fighting, a brawl at a time like this could only lead to trouble.

Yukari fastened her suit, which she had opened to let her skin breathe, and pulled back the curtain covering the kayuta. The lights in the core module were still dimmed for sleep. She was alone.

Light streamed through the open door leading to the docking port. Maybe they were in Kvant-2.

Yukari pushed out of the kayuta and drifted in the direction of the voices. The docking port formed a cross, with the Kvant-2 module above, Kristall below, and Kristall-2 straight ahead. The source of the light was above her.

As Yukari reached the docking port, the voices fell quiet. Had they heard her?

She hesitated for an instant before realizing how foolish she was acting. She was only going to step in to mediate—there was no need to hide.

She heard Nikolai's voice again, softer than a moment before, ingratiating.

Yukari poked her head into the module and froze. Nikolai and Oleg were locked in an embrace. They were kissing.

Yukari's wristwatch clattered against a pipe. The two cosmonauts quickly turned away from each other and faced her. They had both turned beet red.

Nikolai moved first. He pushed off Oleg, propelling himself toward Yukari, his blood-darkened face contorted into a hideous grin.

Yukari was terrified. What kind of trouble had she gotten herself in?

Nikolai grasped Yukari by the shoulder, but she struggled free. Her fight-or-flight response had kicked in, and she was taking flight—but to where?

She raced through the docking port, turning ninety degrees as she rushed into another module—Kristall-2. To her surprise, she found her helmet and backpack secured to the wall ahead of her with velcro—she was at the air lock.

Yukari turned to see Nikolai's massive body blocking the hatch back to the docking port.

"Easy, Yukari. Calm down."

But Yukari was way past calm. She yanked her helmet and backpack off the wall and dove into the air lock.

"Wait! What are you doing?" cried Nikolai.

Ignoring him, Yukari began to turn the handle. The inner hatch caught Nikolai's finger as it closed, but Yukari didn't stop. Nikolai howled in pain, but somehow he managed to work his hand free. The hatch snapped closed. After ensuring it was locked, Yukari hurriedly put on her helmet and backpack.

"What's going on? Where's Yukari?" Oleg was only a few seconds behind Nikolai.

"She's in the air lock. We can't open it from this side."

"What does she think she's doing?" Oleg grabbed on to the inner hatch and knocked loudly. There was no reply. "She's going to get herself killed!"

"We need to cut power to the air lock controls," said Nikolai. "That will prevent the valve vent interlock from actuating. Then we can talk to her over the intercom."

"Let's go!"

Nikolai and Oleg raced to the core module. There in one corner was the power relay panel. A tangled skein of thick cables spilled out when they opened the panel.

"What the—what happened here?" asked Oleg.

"That's right. This was repaired two years ago after the power failure."

"Is this your work?"

"No. Vladimir and Viktor were on board then."

"What do we do? Is there a report detailing the repairs?"

"It's somewhere in Kvant-1 with the rest of the junk."

"We could search for a week and never find it in there! Maybe we should radio TsUP."

"The only people there now are the night watch. They won't know anything about this. You're an engineer—can't you look at the wiring and figure something out?"

Oleg clucked his tongue. "That may be fastest." He brought out a toolbox and got down to work.

The power relay was the heart of the space station. All sixteen kilowatts of power provided by the station's massive solar arrays passed through the relay before being distributed to the batteries, inverters, and countless pieces of equipment on the station.

Sweat beaded on Oleg's forehead.

The repair work on the cables had been crude at best, and the intervening years had left the insulation tape brittle and stiff. In addition, the breakers and fuses had been bypassed, so there was no telling what would happen if Oleg made a wrong move.

"We've been living in a minefield." A terminal caught Oleg's eye. "Cutting this should do it—probably." Oleg took a pair of nippers from the tool kit.

"Not so fast. 'Probably' isn't good enough," protested Nikolai. "You need to be sure."

"We don't have time. It's now or never."

"Does this girl mean that much to you?"

"Please." Oleg turned around, a weary look on his face. "I am not your personal property, Nikolai. I accepted your love, true. And I accept it even now. But this is something I do of my own free will. Freely, you understand?"

"Then why do you seem so happy to see her?"

"I was just being nice to the girl. What is strange about this?"

"Nothing. I only feared you might be…swinging back to the way you were before."

"You're letting yourself get carried away. Again. How many

times have I told you this?"

Oleg looked away from the fuming Nikolai and went back to his work. Impatiently, he put his nippers to one cable. "And do not worry. This will work fine."

Snik.

Then, an explosion in the distance.

[ACT 6]

YUKARI HEARD A tremendous bang, and her body slammed against the inner hatch. At the same instant, the lights on the air lock control panel went out, and Yukari was plunged into darkness.

"Oww! What was that?"

Yukari heard air leaking from somewhere nearby. Hurriedly she put on her helmet and lowered the visor. Turning on the light on her skinsuit, she spun to face the air lock controls—which were written in Cyrillic. She couldn't read a word, and Oleg hadn't bothered explaining the air lock's emergency controls.

"We're moving..."

The impulse that set the station in motion was large. The force of the acceleration would be enough to rip Mir apart at the seams.

Yukari shuddered.

The Russians had been trying to kill her, but something must have gone terribly wrong. It was the only explanation.

Yukari turned her attention to getting out of the air lock. She had no intention of staying on a sinking ship. If she could get back to *Tampopo*, she could buy herself another two hours.

Yukari rotated the handle on the outer hatch. As the hatch opened, air began to spill out. The black gulf of space did the rest of the work for her, forcing the hatch open.

The tether Nikolai had used to secure *Tampopo* was nearby. Yukari's eyes followed the cable to its end, then froze.

"*Tampopo*...it's gone!"

The tether ended abruptly several meters from the air lock. Yukari leaned out and looked around. She froze again.

"Where's Mir?"

[ACT 7]

THE EMERGENCY CALL from TsUP came at 11:40 AM Solomon Islands time, the day after the launch.

"What do you mean Mir is breaking up?" Director Nasuda shouted into the phone. "I want answers, and I want them now!"

"We don't know what's happened yet. All of the station's systems are off-line, and the explosive bolts connecting the Kristall-2 module have fired."

"What kind of death trap are you people trying to pass off as a space station?"

"Each module is designed so it can be jettisoned in the event of an emergency. At this stage we're not sure why that's happened."

"What about Yukari? Is she all right?"

"Yukari...Yukari was in Kristall-2 when it was jettisoned."

"What?" Director Nasuda went pale. "Then get out there and rescue her! Your cosmonauts, they're still alive?"

"They underwent rapid decompression and suffered some burns, but they survived. They're evacuating in the Soyuz capsule now. Yukari was in her space suit at the time of the incident, so there's a chance she's still alive too."

"You have to send your Soyuz to pick her up."

"That is impossible."

"Why?"

"The Soyuz has only enough fuel for the return trip. Even if she were right on top of them, you know how much fuel it takes to make a rendezvous."

"All you have to do is get her back to Mir. The next ship can bring them back."

"We don't know what condition Mir is in. And even if we wanted to do an inspection, Nikolai and Oleg boarded the Soyuz without their space suits. With Mir off the table, we have to bring the Soyuz home."

"Dammit!" Director Nasuda slammed the phone down.

"Yukari already used up twenty minutes of her backpack during the EVA," said Kinoshita. "That leaves forty minutes. An hour if we stretch it."

"Can we send the third ship to get her?"

Kinoshita nodded. "It'll be close...We can just make a rendezvous. But without someone at the controls, we won't be able to dock. If Mir can't guide us in, the closest we can get is a couple of kilometers."

Yukari's space suit wasn't equipped with thrusters, so they would have to pull up right on top of her.

"*Hoi*, then I can pilot the ship," said Matsuri. "I just need to find Kristall-2 and take Yukari back to Mir. She can hold on to the outside of the capsule."

"But we don't even know if Mir is safe," said Director Nasuda.

"The Soyuz can hold one more."

"It's no good. The Soyuz doesn't have an air lock, so they'd have to let the air out of the capsule to bring Yukari aboard, and the cosmonauts don't have space suits."

"Right now, our only option is to use Mir as a lifeboat," said Kinoshita. "It will take fifteen minutes to get Matsuri on board and launch the rocket, then another thirty to rendezvous if we wait until perigee for the main booster burn. Unorthodox, but it should work."

"Can the main booster handle that?"

"Absolutely," said Motoko. "It has an idle burn mode."

"When did you add that?" asked Director Nasuda. Brushing his own question aside, he continued. "You're up, Matsuri. Sorry for the short notice. Satsuki, get her suited up and on the launchpad."

[ACT 8]

YUKARI DRIFTED ALONGSIDE Kristall-2. From out here, the module resembled a large concrete mixer.

They had jettisoned the whole module—but why? Had it been accidental or intentional? Were they really trying to kill her?

Yukari considered the possibility of some international plot, but then it occurred to her that the cosmonauts would not have had time to get directives from their government. So had they tried to kill her just to keep their sex lives private?

It didn't seem likely, but she had no way of knowing now.

She tried the wireless transmitter on her backpack, but there was no answer. She hadn't expected one anyway. The signal was very weak. All long-distance communications had to be routed through *Tampopo*.

Yukari felt her chest tighten. She looked down at the darkened earth below her, hoping she would get one last glimpse of the blue ocean. Nighttime only lasted thirty-five minutes at this orbit— she just wasn't sure if she had that much oxygen.

Her heart leapt momentarily when she looked up and noticed

a glowing red fringe on the outer shell of the Kristall-2, until she decided she wasn't seeing the first light of dawn but the impact of thinly dispersed oxygen molecules against the metal hull.

"Looks like St. Elmo's fire," Yukari muttered to herself. "I thought that was supposed to signal the end of a storm."

Yukari's thoughts drifted until she saw an arc of light appear around the edge of the earth ahead of her. This time, dawn was breaking for real. The light grew until she could see a reddish glow paint the tops of the clouds and blue returning to the ocean.

She turned her eyes away from the suddenly brilliant light and noticed that she was surrounded by innumerable glowing particles, winking at her even in the vacuum of space.

It's the star children, come for me… Yukari thought, her mind drifting into a fog. She felt a sensation as if someone were hugging her.

"*Hoi*, Yukari! You alive in there?"

"Kind of." *Don't spoil the mood, Matsuri. This is just getting good.*

Yukari shook her head. "Huh?" She looked over her shoulder and saw Matsuri with a capsule floating behind her. "What're you doing here?"

"Taking you back to Mir, that's what."

"Mir's okay?"

"Not sure. Guess we'll have to go see. I brought an extra backpack, so let's swap yours out. Then you'll have to hang on to the capsule's nose."

"Oh—okay!" Yukari wasted no time in attaching the fresh backpack.

The oxygenated air hit her like a blast of ice water, and her mind began to race, wondering how launch control had managed to get the third ship up here so quickly. It was very nearly a theoretical impossibility.

Yet she looked at the side of the capsule and there it was—the nickname *Coconut* that Matsuri had given it.

"Getting ready to fire thrusters here, Yukari. You good?" Matsuri asked from inside the capsule. Yukari was straddling the cone of the capsule like it was a horse.

"I'm good. Keep it gentle."

"*Hoi.*"

The capsule began to move. Gradually, they left the drifting fragments of Kristall-2 behind. Yukari waved goodbye to the star children, then turned toward the bright point of light shining in space ahead of them. "That Mir?"

"Yup. Or so Space Command tells me. We've got another thirty kilometers or so to go."

"What happened to the two cosmonauts?"

"They're in the Soyuz. They don't know what's happened to Mir either."

Yukari frowned. She considered trying to contact the Soyuz on her radio but was hesitant. They were close enough to Mir to make out its shape when the Soyuz contacted them.

"You read, Yukari?"

It was Nikolai's voice.

Yukari tensed, then answered, "I read you," as calmly as she could manage.

"We are sorry about what has happened. I did not intend to frighten you. I…can look scary at times."

Yukari listened in silence.

"We were trying to keep you from accidentally going outside, but we made an error and activated the module separation mechanism by mistake."

"I…see."

"Yukari, you must listen closely. If you see any light inside Mir through her windows, then there is a chance you can seek shelter there. If there is no light, then fixing the station is beyond our current capabilities."

"Okay."

"In that case, you will have to board the Soyuz. Know that we do not have space suits, so once you are aboard we will not be able to pilot the capsule for you."

"Excuse me? What?"

"I have entered the return sequence into the computer. As long as you are able to communicate with the ground, you should be fine."

The meaning of what the Russian was saying gradually dawned on her. "Wait...no. Your offer is declined!"

"You *must* accept, Yukari. Oleg feels this as strongly as I do. It is a matter of our pride as cosmonauts."

"But, but I'm—" Yukari gritted her teeth. "I'm an astronaut too! If it's a question of one person dying or two, I *know* the answer!"

"Yukari, you are still young." Nikolai's calm voice sounded in the speaker next to her ear. "We will not steal your future away from you. Especially considering the likely contribution you will make to space exploration."

"But this will be my only flight."

"This I doubt very much. Now, you are close enough to Mir. What do you see? Are there lights in any of the windows?"

Yukari strained her eyes. Not even the faintest pinprick of light came from within the space station.

"Yukari?"

"Nothing. It's completely dark," she said, her voice choking.

"Very well. Bring your craft alongside our Soyuz. We will be draining our air shortly."

"No, Nikolai! Please, don't!"

"*Hoi*, Nikolai?" It was Matsuri, her calm voice seeming almost comically out of place after Yukari's panicked tension.

"What is it?"

"I've thought of a way to get Yukari into my capsule. Then we can all go back home."

"You are sure?"

"That's impossible, Matsuri!"

"No, no, it'll work. I think. Trust me!"

The hatch on the capsule opened. Matsuri was inside, stooped over, fiddling with some equipment.

"What are you planning, Matsuri?"

"First, I'm getting rid of this," she replied, tossing something out through the hatch. When Yukari saw what it was, she felt her heart stop.

"You can't throw out the instrument panel!"

"Hmm. Still not enough room. Guess the whole electrical system's got to go."

"Whoa! Wait! Don't tear the whole thing apart!"

"Don't worry. It's not that bad. We don't need the computer. We can operate the fuse panel manually."

"Matsuri, this is a reentry capsule you're talking about, not some rowboat—hey!"

Matsuri had removed the entire avionics bay set behind the instrument panel and thrown it out into space where it floated, an irreplaceable jumble of specialized computers and wireless devices.

"That should do it. Come on in, Yukari. Let's go home."

"Matsuri!"

"No, really, I insist. Or would you rather have them take you on board the Soyuz?"

Yukari frowned, faced with a true life-or-death decision.

She had gone through more than her share of training runs where they had simulated computer failure and had them cut circuits and operate the craft manually. You could mostly figure out your attitude and position by using the onboard porthole to look at the land below you. She remembered Mukai saying that all the equipment inside the capsules were stand-alone components. Each one could be removed without harming the rest of the machinery. She just hadn't imagined that *all* of them would be removed at the same time.

Reentry was no walk in the park. An object flying just shy of eight kilometers per second hit the atmosphere like a bug hitting a windshield.

The capsules were equipped with heat-resistant shields capable of withstanding flames as hot as a blowtorch, but if they came in at the wrong angle, the shields wouldn't do them any good, and the capsule would burn to a cinder in the blink of an eye.

Without any transmitters left, even if they managed to survive reentry, they had no way of letting anyone know their position.

Miss their timing by even ten seconds and they'd overshoot their splashdown point by a whole eighty kilometers. Yukari had a hard time believing that a boat or helicopter would be able to spot their capsule—hardly larger than an old phone booth—at that distance. If they didn't land exactly where the rescue team expected them to, there was a good chance they could be lost at sea.

Yukari glanced down at her left wrist. Her only chronograph was her Omega wristwatch. They would have to thread the needle with only this and a few fuse panel switches.

Of course, the Soyuz was still an option.

She shook the thought out of her head as soon as she had it. She wouldn't expose two other people to the vacuum of space just to save her own life.

Yukari made up her mind, by herself. Just like a real astronaut.

"Commander Belyayev. I will be going home in this capsule."

"You are quite sure about this?"

"Just watch us!" Yukari replied with an enthusiasm she didn't feel.

Yukari stuck a foot inside the capsule, and Matsuri grabbed hold and pulled her in.

"Yipes! Tight fit."

"C'mon, you can get in further."

"It's r-really cramped." Yukari had to twist until she was practically sitting on Matsuri in order to get all the way inside.

"Yukari, the hatch."

"Right."

Air filled the capsule, and the two took off their helmets and backpacks, pushing them down by their feet.

"How are we ever going to time the deorbit burn? We have to adjust for load too."

"That'll be your department, Yukari. Just do it like Kinoshita taught you. I'm not really up on all that stuff—though I do have a calculator!"

"Well, that's something."

Yukari pulled the calculator and operation manual from the navigational aid pouch.

"I had them attach an orbital path chart at the end," Matsuri told her. "We're supposed to go down into the Arafura Sea on our second pass."

"That's right...here. We don't have much time, do we." Yukari began furiously punching numbers into the calculator. If she subtracted the weight of the equipment Matsuri had jettisoned from her own body weight, she found that the capsule was now five kilos heavier. She could use that to determine the deorbit burn timings and thrust. "I guess we have to do the burn over Brazil—in another six minutes, nine seconds."

"How's our attitude looking?"

"Fine, I think. Wait a second—my hip's on the control stick." She twisted a little, managing to lift slightly off the stick.

"Yukari, I can't see the porthole from here. You'll have to look at it for me."

"Right..."

And so on they went, down through the long list of procedures and adjustments to be made.

Yukari looked between her watch and the manual as she gave directions. "...Three, two, one, cut engines!"

"*Hoi.*"

"Nitrogen blower, on."

"*Hoi.*"

"Retract OMS nozzle."

"Green light."

"Close OMS bay. Check latches one through four."

"*Hoi.* All green."

It was a major feat for two people to do what a computer did in seconds. As soon as the deorbit burn stopped, the capsule began to descend. Yukari checked the angle of the horizon to make sure their orientation was good.

"Pitch control…plus two."

"*Hoi.*"

"That's too far. Minus one."

"*Hoi.*"

"Just a little more!"

"How's that?"

"Good…I think." Yukari felt her own heart racing. "Can we go ahead and jettison our extra fuel now?"

"Can't check from here. Your call."

If they jettisoned their extra fuel, there wouldn't be any more adjustments to their course. They'd be locked on their current trajectory, for better or for worse. But if they didn't get rid of it, there was a chance it could ignite from the heat of reentry.

"Let's ditch it. Open valves B5, B6. Quick."

"*Hoi.*"

Yukari felt the first vibration as they entered the atmosphere over Mindanao.

"Here it comes."

Faint at first, the vibrations steadily grew in intensity. Yukari suddenly became aware of Matsuri's chest pressing against her back.

"Matsuri, you okay? I'm not squishing you, am I?"

"No problem here."

"Okay, but—wait!"

It dawned on Yukari that pressures during reentry climbed to as high as 10 G. Their bodies together would weigh as much as eight hundred kilograms—and Matsuri was on the bottom!

"What are we going to do, Matsuri!? You're going to be a pancake!"

"No worries. We Taliho women are built tough."

"But still—"

The g-forces relentlessly increased. The window was already red with heat. Yukari panicked, but there was nothing she could do. She couldn't even move. There wasn't any space in the capsule that wasn't directly on top of Matsuri. "No! I'm going to crush you!"

"No, you won't."

"Yes, I will!"

"Dad—" Matsuri seemed to be having trouble breathing. "Dad told me to look out for you, s-so don't…worry…"

"Hey! No! Mat—"

An incredible rumbling vibration drowned out Yukari's voice as the g-forces enveloped the capsule. Yukari felt herself being pressed down into Matsuri's body. She tried to brace herself with her arms, but they were pinned by her sides.

After three minutes that felt like an eternity, the weight finally lifted.

Yukari called Matsuri's name over and over, but there was no response.

"What is it with everybody sacrificing themselves? You're not allowed to do that, okay? You're not allowed to die!"

The capsule shot downward like an arrow, and Yukari wept until the last corner of her rational mind remembered something she had to do.

Yukari groped for the fuse panel, found the switch to deploy the parachute, and threw it. She felt several quick impacts as the capsule passed through the cloud layer, and the main chute opened only moments before they hit the surface of the water. After the floats had fully deployed, Yukari threw open the hatch and crawled out into the bright sunlight on the surface of the hull.

Crouching, she reached back into the capsule and undid Matsuri's harness, giving her a shake.

"Matsuri! Wake up!" Yukari wiped at her eyes and stared at her sister's face. "Matsuri…"

Matsuri's eyelashes twitched. Then her eyelids opened, and she stared straight up at Yukari with her large, catlike eyes. "*Hoi?* Yukari? Where are we?"

"Earth," Yukari said with a sob. "We're home."

The sky and sea were blue as far as the eye could see. There was no land in sight. The two girls sat side by side on the capsule, feet in the water, letting the salty wind blow through their hair.

That blue, Yukari thought. *It's the same deep, equatorial, vibrant blue.*

"You know," she said, "we may not be too far off our splash-down point after all."

Matsuri smiled. "I think you may be right."

It was only a few moments later that they heard the whine from the turbines of an approaching helicopter.

[ACT 9]

BY THE END of the year, Maltide was the center of a worldwide media frenzy.

Director Nasuda's announcement of a seven-figure price for a manned space mission that would have cost the space shuttle nine figures to pull off had shaken the space industry.

The cost of building satellites dropped like a stone now that follow-up maintenance was a real possibility. No longer did a company have one chance only to make a satellite that would never fail. This also brought down soaring satellite insurance premiums, cutting overall program costs by a third.

When the economic impact of the Solomon Space Association became clear, the Japanese government backed off their earlier threats of funding cuts and doubled funding for the coming year.

For Yukari and Matsuri, the media attention meant instant international stardom. But Yukari refused all the banquet invitations and parade plans, instead choosing to focus on getting ready for her return to school the following semester. Director Nasuda literally groveled at her feet to give at least one press conference, but she was unmovable.

She had had enough of parties.

What changed her mind was a short international phone call from her mother that came the day before she was to return to Japan.

"Your school found out about your job," her mother told her. "You've been expelled."

Expelled? Nearly a fate worse than dying alone in space!
Be sure to check out what happens next in
Rocket Girls: The Last Planet.

AFTERWORD

WHEN *ROCKET GIRLS* was first published in 1995, it was hailed as a "prophetic" book foretelling what tomorrow held for space exploration. The book became so popular, in fact, that it quickly became hard to find on bookstore shelves. I cannot express how delighted I am that *Rocket Girls* is now available to an English-speaking audience, and it is my great hope that some of those involved with the space programs of North America and Europe will keep the book close at hand and find it a useful reference as they plan for the future.

So, what warrants the "prophetic" label *Rocket Girls* has earned? When the book was updated in 2007 to coincide with the release of the anime version, I addressed this very question in the afterword, excerpts of which follow.

1. The second space shuttle disaster led to a period of greatly reduced manned spaceflight.

Director Nasuda discusses this at the beginning of the book. NASA was forced to rely on the Russians to ferry astronauts to the International Space Station. At the time, the Russian workforce itself had been decimated, leaving both programs in a precarious position.

2. Manned spaceflight using hybrid rockets is a reality.

This incredible achievement was accomplished by a private company led by the brilliant Burt Rutan. This novel portrays a similar example of a small group of talented individuals working together to accomplish an ambitious goal.

Unlike the rocket described in the book, the actual hybrid is only capable of suborbital flight; greater thrust is probably necessary to reach orbital velocity. However, since this is a work of science fiction, we can make up the difference.

3. NASA's next generation spacecraft will employ a capsule design.

NASA has learned from the high cost and safety problems of the space shuttle. In light of this, it's safe to dismiss criticism of this book for using a "primitive" capsule design. NASA is planning two new launch vehicles: Ares I, which will loft the crew into orbit, and Ares V, which will carry cargo. This is the same, eminently rational, division of labor envisioned in the book.

4. Skintight space suits have entered the research phase.

Even I had doubts that this would become a reality. Nonetheless, JAXA's own literature now makes mention of "skintight" space suits, and research on their design is underway in laboratories at MIT. An Internet search for "bio-suit" will bring up the website, which describes the suit much as it appears in the book—a "second skin." There's even a picture of a mock-up suit that looks exactly like Yukari's skinsuit.

It will probably be some time before the suit is ready for use, but when it is, it will give a significant edge to manned spaceflight. Current space suits significantly restrict motion, making robots much more competitive in this area than they otherwise would be.

Three years ago, I ended the afterword here. Have there been any developments in the intervening years that would add to that list? Read on.

5. The dawn of private-sector space exploration.

Space X, a company created by one of the founders of PayPal, has succeeded in launching its Falcon 1 and Falcon 9 rockets. In Hokkaido, Takafumi Horie, a popular figure in the IT industry, is conducting experiments on liquid-fueled rockets. Though their plans closely resemble one another, they were conceived independently. Still another private developer in Hokkaido has created a small hybrid rocket by the name of CAMUI, which is now available commercially.

You might be wondering how this qualifies as prophetic. Wasn't the Solomon Space Association backed by government funding?

Though this is true, the management at the SSA as depicted in the book is decidedly private sector. They didn't choose the Solomon Islands for their base simply because the site was ideal for launching rockets. They also wanted a location where they would be free of government intervention and bureaucracy, while at the same time affording them some degree of economic independence.

That so many successful figures from the IT industry have stepped forward to meet the challenges posed by space exploration indicates to me that, free to apply their own resources to the task, they feel they stand a chance of outdoing NASA. And as it happens, NASA appears to agree. The agency has already begun working in partnership with many of these private projects. Space X tested Falcon 1 on an island no one had ever heard of, while Falcon 9 launched from Cape Canaveral. NASA is also supporting the development of Space X's manned *Dragon* capsule, while at the same time canceling its own Ares program, mentioned above in point 3.

In fact, even I am working as a fellow in the space exploration division of an IT firm. I envision a bright future for mankind where ordinary people can travel easily between Earth and space. I believe we must strive to make the world depicted in *Rocket Girls* a reality, so that one day even husky individuals like me will be able to enjoy the thrill of space travel.

Housuke Nojiri
June 2010

ABOUT THE AUTHOR

Born in Mie, Japan, in 1961. After working in instrumentation control, CAD programming, and video game design, Housuke Nojiri published his first work, *The Blind Spot of Veis*, based on the video game *Creguian*, in 1992. He gained popularity with his subsequent works the *Creguian* series and the *Rocket Girl* series. In 2002, he published *Usurper of the Sun*, ushering in a new era of space science fiction in Japan. After first appearing as a series of short stories, *Usurper* won the Seiun Award for best Japanese science fiction novel of 2002 and was published in English in 2009. His other works include *Pendulum of Pinieru* and *Fuwa-Fuwa no Izumi*.

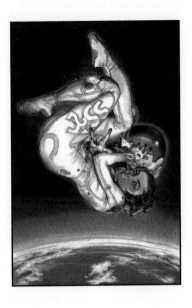

Coming soon from Haikasoru!
ROCKET GIRLS: THE LAST PLANET

When the Rocket Girls accidentally land in the yard of Yukari Morita's old school, it looks as though their experiment is ruined. Luckily, the geeky Akane is there to save the day. Fitting the profile—she's intelligent, enthusiastic, and petite—Akane is soon recruited by the Solomon Space Association. Yukari and Akane are then given the biggest Rocket Girl mission yet: a voyage to the edge of the solar system and the minor planet of Pluto to save a NASA probe.

HAIKASORU
THE FUTURE IS JAPANESE

HARMONY BY PROJECT ITOH

In the future, Utopia has finally been achieved thanks to medical nanotechnology and a powerful ethic of social welfare and mutual consideration. This perfect world isn't that perfect though, and three young girls stand up to totalitarian kindness and super-medicine by attempting suicide via starvation. It doesn't work, but one of the girls—Tuan Kirie—grows up to be a member of the World Health Organization. As a crisis threatens the harmony of the new world, Tuan rediscovers another member of her suicide pact, and together they must help save the planet…from itself.

THE OUROBOROS WAVE BY JYOUJI HAYASHI

Ninety years from now, a satellite detects a nearby black hole scientists dub Kali after the Hindu goddess of destruction. Humanity embarks on a generations-long project to tap the energy of the black hole and establish colonies on planets across the solar system. Earth and Mars and the moons Europa (Jupiter) and Titania (Uranus) develop radically different societies, with only Kali, that swirling vortex of destruction and creation, and the hated but crucial Artificial Accretion Disk Development association (AADD) in common.

SUMMER, FIREWORKS, AND MY CORPSE BY OTSUICHI

Two short novels, including the title story and *Black Fairy Tale*, plus a bonus short story. *Summer* is a simple story of a nine-year-old girl who dies while on summer vacation. While her youthful killers try to hide her body, she tells us the story—from the point of view of her dead body—of the children's attempt to get away with murder. *Black Fairy Tale* is classic J-horror: a young girl loses an eye in an accident, but receives a transplant. Now she can see again, but what she sees out of her new left eye is the experiences and memories of its previous owner. Its previous *deceased* owner.

Also by Housuke Nojiri—**USURPER OF THE SUN**

Aki Shiraishi is a high school student working in the astronomy club and one of the few witnesses to an amazing event—someone is building a tower on the planet Mercury. Soon, the enigmatic Builders have constructed a ring around the sun, and the ecology of Earth is threatened by its immense shadow. Aki is inspired to pursue a career in science, and the truth. She must determine the purpose of the ring and the plans of its creators, as the survival of both species—humanity and the alien Builders—hangs in the balance.

VISIT US AT WWW.HAIKASORU.COM